CIRCUS
EXTRAORDINAIRE

EPHEMIA
RIMALDI

Red Deer Press

LINDA DEMEULEMEESTER

Published in Canada by Red Deer Press,
209 Wicksteed Avenue, Unit 51, Toronto, ON   M4G 0B1.

Published in the United States by Red Deer Press,
60 Leo M Birmingham Pkwy, Ste 107, Brighton, MA 02135.

Library and Archives Canada Cataloguing in Publication
Title: Ephemia Rimaldi : circus performer extraordinaire / written by Linda
DeMeulemeester.
Names: DeMeulemeester, Linda, 1956- author.
Identifiers: Canadiana 20230228364 | ISBN 9780889957299 (softcover)
Classification: LCC PS8607.E58 E64 2023 | DDC jC813/.6—dc23

Publisher Cataloging-in-Publication Data (U.S.)
Names: DeMeulemeester, Linda, 1956-, author.
Title: Ephemia Rimaldi: Circus Performer Extraordinaire / Linda DeMeulemeester.
Description: Toronto, Ontario : Red Deer Press, 2023. | Summary: "Set on the
eve of the 20th century, when female performers were one of the earliest groups
to demand equal pay for equal work, this historical adventure offers important
themes for today's readers. The suffragist movement and early circus life serve
as a backdrop for a feisty heroine who champions equality for all. Themes
include social justice, agency, forgiveness and respect for diversity"-- Provided
by publisher.
Identifiers: ISBN 978-0-88995-729-9 (paperback)
Subjects: LCSH Circus performers — Juvenile fiction. | Women -- Suffrage --
Juvenile fiction. | Social justice – Juvenile fiction. | Historical fiction. | BISAC:
JUVENILE FICTION / Girls & Women. | JUVENILE FICTION / Social Themes
/ Activism & Social Justice.
Classification: LCC PZ7.D468Ep | DDC 813.6 – dc23

Red Deer Press acknowledges with thanks the Canada Council for the Arts and the
Ontario Arts Council for their support of our publishing program. We acknowledge
the financial support of the Government of Canada through the Canada Book Fund (CBF)
for our publishing activities.

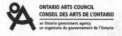

Edited for the Press by Beverley Brenna
Text and cover design by Tanya Montini
Copyedit by Penny Hozy
Printed in Canada by Copywell

For Mitch, Emily,
Amanda, Mikel,
and
Maddy!

CHAPTER ONE

DAUGHTERS OF FREEDOM

Effy ducked as a cabbage sailed past her head. An egg flew over her shoulder and smashed against the brick building behind her. Egg splattered on the sleeve of her first fitted dress, which was the colour of a spring meadow. She had begged Aunt Ada for this dress, and now egg glistened like a slug trail along her silk sleeve. Effy's blood boiled.

"Only bad women want to vote!" shouted the man in a bowler hat. This time he threw a tomato, and it landed by Effy's boot.

"Go home to your dollies, little girl."

Effy put down her protest sign. Scooping up the dripping tomato from the cobbled street, she chucked it back into the crowd, aiming for that hat. The red muck landed successfully on the man's forehead, and tomato juice dripped down his plump cheeks. He shook his fist at her as his face turned crimson and then purple. His cigar slid out of his mouth and plunked onto the ground.

Effy decided in a snap that she wouldn't avoid the truth of it. While it was disgraceful behaviour—hitting the man with a tomato—it was one of her most satisfying moments. She didn't give a fig about her tomato-slimed glove, either. She grabbed her sign and scurried away to join her great-aunt at the front of the protest march on Bloor Street.

"Ephemia Rimaldi, where did you get to?" said Aunt Ada in huffs and puffs. Despite her advanced age, her great-aunt was a boundless bundle of energy in matters of changing the world.

Effy didn't say. Instead, she raised her sign and kept marching.

"Do you hear what some people in the crowd are shouting?" asked Letitia Nettles, when she'd pushed through the marching women and taken her place beside Effy's aunt. "They're saying one of our protesters assaulted a man with a tomato."

Effy's cheeks burned. She stopped and turned around, hoping she looked only curious and not a smidge guilty.

"Ephemia, hold your placard up high and proud," Aunt Ada scolded her.

Effy hoisted her "Votes for Women" sign, even though the wood handle kept sliding through her tomato-slimed glove. She quickly pulled off her glove and let its guilty evidence drop among their marching feet.

As the other protesters chanted—"Simple Equality" and "From Prison to Citizenship"—Effy made sure she shouted above all the others. Almost thirteen, Ephemia Rimaldi needed to show her great-aunt that she was ready to join her first public protest.

Effy had spent the last year assisting her aunt with the printing press in the cellar. She folded and handed out women's suffrage leaflets. Effy also served tea and plates of biscuits at her aunt's important ladies' meetings, where they discussed how they would win the vote.

Finding her place in Aunt Ada's household had been no easy journey. Effy's father, a scoundrel, a flimflammer, and worse, circus riffraff, had abandoned her at birth. She'd been passed amongst her mother's farming relatives, only to be called, "too stubborn," or "too difficult," or worst of all, "too sassy." At the age of eleven, she was finally deposited with Aunt Ada in Toronto.

Great-aunt Ada, the sternest, most intimidating Rimaldi, was getting on in years and could use some assistance. No one in the Rimaldi family actually wanted to tell her that. Instead, Aunt Ada was told that Effy had her poppa's bad blood, and she'd come to no good unless a firm hand was taken.

Aunt Ada had grand plans to educate her unmanageable niece. Effy declared it was as if she'd been a parched traveller, stumbling in the desert, who'd been led to an oasis of books. Effy and Aunt Ada quickly realized they were a perfect match.

Effy and the protestors marched past a billboard advertising a circus at Toronto's exhibition grounds. Effy slowed and stared at the picture of a man on a swinging trapeze.

"Ephemia, keep up the pace," said Aunt Ada.

Perhaps other girls her age were eagerly waiting to see acrobats and tigers, but Effy kept her mind on important business. On the edge of the great new century, women needed the vote and to win more rights. Aunt Ada had told her that women needed simple equality.

Effy was fine with that notion. She wanted to go to college, something boys were allowed to do, but only a few privileged women. Society didn't approve of higher education for girls. But Effy knew her great-Aunt Ada would help her succeed.

Aunt Ada encouraged Effy. She'd enrolled Effy in an academy and set aside a trust fund for all future tuition. That left no time for watching circuses or playing with dollies.

Close behind Effy, a woman screamed. The crowd broke into a roar. Effy turned and saw police constables astride tall brown horses, ploughing through the protestors. A brute of a man knocked over one of the marchers; her straw hat flopped sideways and slipped off her head. Effy's heart thudded against her rib cage. The poor woman scrambled to her feet, thankfully, but she did not get away. One of the constables arrested her.

"Aunt Ada." Effy kept looking over her shoulder. "I think we should get out of here."

"There is no rebirth without pain, Ephemia," said Aunt Ada.

"There is no accomplishment without sacrifice," chirped Miss Letitia.

"And we must never fail in our nerve, but always show our grit and determination." Effy croaked this as her throat closed in. "But can't we be determined not to get arrested?"

Effy tugged her aunt's arm and forced her to turn around. Aunt Ada's eyes widened in alarm as she saw protestors being pushed and shoved, struggling as they were dragged to the ground by constables. Some men in the crowd were jeering, and other men and women were shouting at the police to leave the protesters alone. Fistfights broke out.

"Perhaps it is best we're able to protest another day," mused Aunt Ada.

The front lines of women broke up quickly, but the brigade of mounted police charged toward them. Effy dropped her protest sign and pushed Aunt Ada into a narrow cobbled lane. Miss Letitia followed them.

There were more shouts and fighting, and Effy, who had never seen violence up close, felt her eyes blur. She could barely make out the shape of Aunt Ada pressed up against a doorway, breathing heavily.

Aunt Ada straightened her straw boater's hat and stiffened her spine. "No time for tears, Ephemia. We must make haste while the wind is at our backs."

Together, Effy and Miss Letitia assisted Aunt Ada as they ran through the laneways.

"Dear, oh, dear," cried Miss Letitia as she stepped in a pile of rubbish. "What if there are rats?"

"They'd be smaller than the rats that are chasing us," Effy said through her teeth. She let go of her aunt's hand and ducked under a ladder set against a brick wall. Aunt Ada let out a shriek. Effy froze, thinking a police constable was about to smack her with a billy club, or run her over with his horse.

Then Aunt Ada gasped, "Ephemia, never walk under

a ladder. You know it is terrible bad luck."

Effy drew in a calming breath and said, "It would only be unlucky if the ladder fell on me." She could hear the clip-clop of horses in the street behind. "And if we don't hurry, worse luck is on the way."

Effy, Miss Letitia, and Aunt Ada crossed Queen's Park and wound their way through twisting streets, until they finally reached their own respectable neighbourhood. Only then did Aunt Ada stop and catch her breath in gasps and wheezes. Mopping her head with her handkerchief, she straightened her hat. At Effy's suggestion, they slipped off their gold suffragist sashes and tucked them away. When they strolled under the elm trees and past the stately Victorian houses, it was as if they were returning from a church picnic.

Safely inside her home, Aunt Ada flopped heavily onto her wingback chair in the parlour. "Ephemia, my nitroglycerine, please," she said weakly.

Effy fumbled in Aunt Ada's drawstring bag and produced a tiny white tablet. Aunt Ada placed it on her tongue. Miss Letitia took out her handkerchief and flapped it uselessly in front of Aunt Ada's face. Aunt Ada brushed it away as if it were an annoying mosquito.

Some colour returned to Aunt Ada's cheeks. "Good

grief, that was rather unexpected. Imagine us being chased like common criminals." She woefully shook her head. "Why, we now have telegraph machines that send messages across the world in seconds, and streetcars rushing along city streets at dangerous speeds of fifteen miles per hour. But politicians can't get it through their thick skulls that women should win the vote?"

Miss Letitia nodded. "Women need to get into politics and make sure morals don't slide in these fast times. It is our duty to steer society in the right direction."

"What direction would that be?" Effy wondered out loud. "We want to make our own choices. Surely not so we can then tell others what they can or can't do."

"Quite the contrary," Miss Letitia sniffed. "We are moral guardians who must stamp out demon rum and fight social ills."

"I thought we were marching so I could go to college?" Effy's face flushed, realizing how selfish that sounded. "I mean ..."

"I know perfectly well what you mean, Ephemia." Aunt Ada still sounded quite out of breath. "Don't forget, we each must serve a greater calling than just worrying about ourselves. Only when we open up the university doors to more women than those of refined society can *all* women advance."

Effy had printed flyers for the suffragists. Local papers complained that demanding equal rights only stirred women up. Knowing her aunt's friends, Effy believed women were already stirred.

Aunt Ada leaned forward, held Effy's gaze, and furrowed her brow. "You'll soon need to settle on *your* one true purpose."

Effy was about to tell her aunt that she had no idea what that purpose might be. So, until then, couldn't she focus on her education? Only her aunt said, "Ephemia, would you please make me a pot of tea. I am in great need of libation to ease my dry throat."

"Of course." Effy hurried to the kitchen as Miss Letitia bid her farewell.

"She is willful and selfish," Effy overheard Miss Letitia say.

"She is determined and focused," contradicted Aunt Ada. "And she has a sharp mind. She'll need all that to blaze a trail to success. I believe it is my true purpose to make sure my niece goes to college."

The door banged shut after Miss Letitia bid goodbye.

Effy promised under her breath that she'd never let

Aunt Ada down. Still, she snorted as she pumped water into the kettle and lit a flame for the stove. *Selfish and willful ... but at least Aunt Ada understood.* All Effy wanted was to choose her own direction. She certainly hadn't got far when others had been in charge.

A girl needs a say in her own destiny. But good luck, getting anyone to listen. Even Aunt Ada hadn't consulted Effy, but it worked out because they were of like minds regarding Effy's going to school. Why, if it was up to the rest of her family, she'd still be washing laundry, sweeping, and scrubbing floors. Not to mention, instead of attending the academy this fall, she'd be at her other auntie's farm, digging carrots and potatoes out of the dirt all the livelong day.

Aunt Ada had been scandalized by Effy's spotty education and had arranged a tutor. In turn, Effy had worked hard and was ready for the academy.

Wasn't that what the suffragist movement was all about—freedom? What did she care what others chose for themselves?

When the kettle whistled, Effy spooned tea leaves into a pot and poured steaming water, all the while figuring out how to remove the egg mess from the delicate material of her dress. Frowning, she pumped a trickle of cold water onto her sleeve and began scraping the silk cloth with her fingernail.

A bang, a tinkle of glass, and then another crash startled her. Black feathers splattered the windowpane. Her first thought was *poor little bird*. Her second thought was *oh, goodness, I can't let Aunt Ada see this*. Grabbing the whisk broom and a dustpan, she flew out the kitchen door and hurried down the wooden steps.

Rimaldis were superstitious, all right. "No point taking any chances," Aunt Ada would say.

A bird flying into a window could be, according to Aunt Ada, the worst of luck. A dead bird meant there'd be a death in the house. Effy shook her head as she looked for the unfortunate bird in the shrubbery.

Effy wasn't superstitious. Wishing on falling stars had never delivered her a loving mother and father and sisters and brothers. So she relied only on reason. Reason such as: what her aunt couldn't see wouldn't upset her.

Effy carefully whisked the bird onto her dustpan. Lifting the dustpan and leaning her ear to the bird's feather-ruffled chest, she made sure the poor little fellow had truly departed to the Great Beyond. Then she buried him in the compost that smelled of grass cuttings and flower petals. She wiped her hands.

Hurrying back into the kitchen, she poured tea into Aunt Ada's favourite china cup. She poured in an extra dollop of milk, as the tea had brewed quite strong. Balancing a saucer to catch the drops of sloshing tea, Effy headed into the parlour and stopped in her tracks.

Rather strangely, what Effy thought of first was that she hadn't found any broken glass in the kitchen or in the yard. She stared at the parlour rug and said, "Oh, that's the crash I heard, a broken lamp."

It was another long second before she realized dear Aunt Ada had also departed to the Great Beyond.

CHAPTER TWO .

WOLVES AT THE DOOR

Aunt Ada had been quite clear what was to happen in the event of her death. With her usual bluntness, she'd say, "After all, Ephemia, I am an old lady."

Effy's aunt believed there should be a proper mourning period. "Because I am also a *rich* old lady, and relatives will be pawing on the porch like wolves at the door."

Only the wolves couldn't wait ...

Uncle Edgar, the eldest brother, declared himself an important and busy man, and decided it was best to dispatch the funeral and the will on the same day. While there was a small turnout at the grave, all the Rimaldis swooped in for the will reading. They perched on their chairs like a murder of crows, the older ones smelling of camphor and mutton.

A bird-like lawyer strutted into the parlour and made himself comfortable at Aunt Ada's desk.

"Do you suppose we might honeymoon in Europe with some of my inheritance?" cousin Hattie asked her fiancé,

Reverend Mason. He straightened his clerical collar and said, "I will decide those things now." Then the reverend patted Hattie's head, *like she's a pet cat*, thought Effy.

Effy chewed on her lip as she sat stiffly in the cane chair. Good posture wasn't difficult, because her jet black dress was so starched, she could barely bend. As the Rimaldis quibbled about windfalls of inheritance money, steam gathered inside Effy like a tea kettle.

Before she exploded, Effy stood and clasped her hands in front of her. Bowing her head, she said, "Perhaps we should take a moment and reflect upon what Great-aunt Ada meant to all of us."

"Your great-aunt squandered our inheritance on trying to win the vote for women and other such nonsense," grumbled Uncle Edgar.

"She devoted her energy to frivolous meetings and marches, and pampering little urchins like you," Aunt Wilhelmina said in a nasally voice.

"Marching in those women's parades ruined our good name," said Cousin Hattie. She turned to her fiancé. "I'm lucky you proposed anyway."

Reverend Mason's gaze was fastened on the will. Effy raised her eyebrows and said, "I doubt it's our family's *reputation* that he cares about."

"You are so ill-mannered, speaking about a parson in that way," said one of the ancient Rimaldis.

Effy opened her mouth and shut it again. Aunt Ada was a great woman. How did they not see that? She slumped back into her chair ... well, she would have slumped, but only her knees would bend in such a stiff dress.

Uncle Edgar patted the pomaded hair glued to his skull and tweaked the tips of his bushy moustache. *He truly does look like a walrus*, decided Effy. Clearing his throat, Uncle Edgar declared, "I will not sell the house or any other property."

The lawyer bobbed his bird-like head in agreement. "This is the law. Property is passed on to the eldest male relative. He may do as he sees fit."

The murmurs rose. The lawyer eyed everyone like they were a nest of wasps ready to attack. Effy reckoned he wasn't wrong.

Reverend Mason stood and crossed his arms. "Wait, Ada would have had money in the bank. She must have left that to us, I mean, to my fiancé."

"Not quite." The lawyer's Adam's apple bobbed up and down. "That part of Ada's money is locked in an education trust fund for one ...

"... **Ephemia Rimaldi** ..."

All eyes turned toward Effy. The angry wasps were about to set upon her. Effy squished herself as far back into her chair as her starched dress would allow.

Aunt Wilhelmina narrowed her eyes and stared at Effy as if she was sizing up a new horse. Effy was surprised she didn't ask to see her teeth.

"I've said time and again, there is no point in educating a girl," complained Uncle Edgar. "How high does she need to count in order to bake bread?"

Effy rolled her eyes.

"Exactly how much is in this trust fund?" asked the reverend.

Uncle Edgar grabbed the bank paper from the lawyer's hand. His eyes bulged, making him look even more walrussy. "Ada must have planned to educate every girl in this city."

"Can't we claim this fund or change it, or ...?" Uncle Edgar sputtered, and the lawyer wiped spittle from his gold-rimmed glasses.

"No." The lawyer darted out of his chair as if he was a fly that Uncle Edgar might swat. "Only her legal *guardian* can do that."

"Legal guardian, you say." Aunt Wilhelmina perked up like a plant that had just been watered. "Well, I suppose we should adopt her, now that Ada's gone. Ephemia, wouldn't you love to come live with me and Uncle Lorenzo?"

"The reverend and I are the logical choice to become Ephemia's guardians," said Hattie, turning to Effy. "Your great-aunt would have wanted it."

Reverend Mason nodded as he whispered to Hattie, "And we'll educate her in manners, while we charge her trust fund for our trouble."

"I'm sitting right here," Effy said to them. "Shouldn't I have a say in what I want?"

"You expect to tell *us* what you need?" The reverend shook his head. "This girl is wicked, through and through," he snapped. "It is our moral duty to become her guardian."

A great sigh erupted from Uncle Walrus. He gripped another paper from the desk. "Ephemia already has a legal guardian," he announced.

Effy's jaw dropped. This was news to her!

"Unfortunately," continued Uncle Edgar, "he is a most confounding and uncooperative scoundrel who couldn't care less about us ... ah, Ephemia."

Aunt Wilhelmina wilted back into her chair. Hattie and her fiancé looked as if they'd bitten into a lemon. Effy could barely breathe. Guardian? Did her uncle mean her ... could it be?

Uncle Edgar hovered over the very desk Effy had leaned on when Aunt Ada checked Effy's homework: fractions and the equation for interest over rate and time. One of Effy's favourite math tasks was calculating compound interest.

"When is the last time her so-called guardian contacted the family?" Uncle Edgar asked.

"According to Ada, never," said Aunt Wilhelmina.

"Ephemia is *abandoned*, then." Uncle Edgar handed the paper to the lawyer. "Do something about this!"

Uncle Edgar turned back to Hattie and Aunt Wilhelmina. "In the meantime, this girl is thirteen. That's old enough to work for a living."

"I'm still twelve." Why was everyone talking about Effy as if she wasn't in the room?

"Twelve is old enough to be a hired girl." Uncle Edgar tugged his moustache. "That's the solution. We'll find Ephemia a job until our lawyer turns the trust fund back to me ... I mean us."

"Aunt Ada's final wish was for me to have a good education. I want that, too," said Effy. Uncle Edgar glared at her, but she refused to look away like the quivering lawyer.

"Oh, you'll come down a peg or two." Uncle Edgar turned away first. "Once you've been shown your place in this world."

"I am going to choose my place," Effy announced through gritted teeth. She may as well have whispered because no one paid the slightest notice.

The lawyer fumbled with his papers. "I don't think breaking the trust will be possible, as long as her guardian ..."

Uncle Edgar scowled and slammed his fist on the desk. "Her guardian could be dead, for all we know."

Effy's heart thudded in her chest.

"I'll look into it, sir." The papers trembled in the lawyer's hands. "The will could be changed if we, ah, find a sympathetic judge. It might take some time, though."

"In the meantime, Ephemia can earn her keep. We'll send her to a distant cousin who runs a boarding house," declared the walrus. "And she can send back her wages because she's causing this trouble."

"That's not going to happen," Effy muttered to no one in particular. The Rimaldis stood and shuffled out of the parlour. They headed for the dining room, where Cousin Hattie had set out a few meager parsley sandwiches and a pot of weak tea.

Effy stayed behind and made her way to the bookshelf. From the bottom shelf, she pulled out the book: *Moby Dick*.

Aunt Ada had once told Effy, "While it's a sin to damage a book, I never cared for this one." Then she showed Effy the hollowed pages and where she'd hidden emergency money. "This entire book was only about a vengeful man and a vengeful whale."

Effy had stared at the book cover. "I'd be angry and fight back if someone was trying to harpoon me."

"You are contrary." Aunt Ada had smiled. "You'll be a good suffragist."

Effy blinked back tears. Then, without a smidge of guilt—well, perhaps a smidge, though this was surely an emergency—Effy folded two bills and grabbed a handful of coins. She stuffed the money in the pocket of her dress. She plucked the paper off the desk and read: **Legal guardian: Phineas Rimaldi. Current address: Somewhere with the Great Rimaldi Circus.**

Scoundrel or not, her poppa hadn't abandoned her. Or, at least, he hadn't given her up, not legally. Effy tucked the paper in the same pocket as her money. She went upstairs to pack her things in her large embroidered bag. She and Aunt Ada had made that bag together. Well, actually, Effy had only embroidered five leaves, because Aunt Ada had kept making her redo the stiches.

They were very fine leaves.

Effy changed out of her mourning clothes and into her most grown-up outfit, the green dress. Its sleeve still had the egg stain. Her suffragist hat, a straw boater, was the final touch. She must look sixteen. Well, at least thirteen. When she crept downstairs, her relatives were still plotting and planning in the parlour. No one noticed her slip out the door.

Effy walked away from the elegant Victorian house on the hill, with its fine furnishings and comfortable life.

She did not look back.

CHAPTER THREE

THE LEAST LIKELY GIRL

Effy Rimaldi considered herself the least likely girl on earth to run away and join a circus. She'd be much more likely to run away and join a bank—if girls were allowed to be bankers.

But life had a way of twisting a person in unexpected directions.

As Effy's relatives sat in the parlour, sipping tea and scheming to steal her trust fund, she rode one of the new streetcars straight to Toronto's exhibition grounds.

The sun beat down on the waterfront. Effy wiped the perspiration from her face and stopped at a ticket booth. Behind the booth, blue-striped circus tents covered the fairground like giant toadstools.

"Excuse me, sir," she said to the ticket seller. "I'm in need of particular circus information. May I please see the person in charge?"

"And who do you suppose that might be?" the man

said with a gap-toothed grin. His bald head, poking from the top of his visor, reminded Effy of a boiled egg in its cup.

Effy shrugged. "I suppose it's the ringmaster." Wafts of roasting peanuts and popped corn drifted from the circus midway. A dull pain thudded behind her eyes, and her throat was parched. She should have eaten one of Cousin Hattie's miserly parsley sandwiches and gulped a cup of tea.

"And I suppose the ringmaster has nothing better to do than run over here while the matinee is on. Buy a ticket or beat it, little girl," said the ticket man.

Little girl? Effy's blood boiled. How could she get him to listen? She considered what Aunt Ada would do and pounded her fist against the ticket ledge. The flimsy booth shook. The ticket seller's jaw dropped.

"Then I need to speak to the next person in charge!" Effy commanded.

The man smiled but not, Effy thought, in a particularly *I'm going to help you* way. "Please," she added.

"That would be the boss-handler," the ticket seller said. "He's the person who really runs the circus and knows what's going on."

Effy stepped aside as a couple of gangly schoolboys tossed their quarters on the ledge. "Two tickets."

The man in the booth swiped the coins into his cash box and handed them two ticket stubs. "This is only for the matinee. Don't think 'cause you've missed the first twenty minutes, you can stay for the evening show."

The boys grumbled and pushed past Effy.

"Well, are you going to bring the boss-handler?" Effy asked.

"Like I said, there's a show going on. He's busy." The ticket seller turned away and counted the cash in his box. When he turned back, he muttered, "Are you still here?"

"You, sir, are a most exasperating man." Effy stamped her foot in the dirt, raising more dust, which coated the bottom of her dress. Sighing, she said, "I must find out where a particular circus is located—specifically, the Rimaldi Circus."

She leaned over the ledge and stared nose-to-nose with the man in the booth. "Someone in this place must know where other circuses are travelling. Otherwise, all the circuses could end up in the same town at the same time."

"That's right calculating, it is," the man said, looking mildly impressed. "You're correct. There are planned circuits. So, what's it worth to you, finding out where this Rimaldi Circus is?"

"Worth? Do you mean I should still pay for a ticket?

That's twenty-five cents!" Effy considered the small sum of dollars and coins in her pocket.

"That's general admission." A sly look crossed the ticket seller's face. "You're asking for specific special information. That costs more."

Tears of frustration stung Effy's eyes, but she sensed the gap-toothed man wasn't the type to melt at a girl's tears. Nor would she be his match for bargaining.

"Fine, name your price." She sighed. "But I have little coin to spare."

The ticket seller glanced at her silk dress, and then down at her gloved hands and kid-leather boots. "What's your game, little girlie?"

What was Effy supposed to say? That she was worried a judge would decide against a trust fund for school? That the family would get her money and send Effy to a boarding house as a hired girl ...?

... That her only *hope* was to locate her long lost poppa?

Instead, Effy said in an exasperated voice, "I am not a 'little girlie,' and this is no game. I'm trying to contact my father in the Rimaldi Circus. It is urgent."

The man raised an eyebrow. "Father! Why didn't ya say so?" He got up and left his booth.

"Wait," said Effy. "I need ..."

"Yes, yes, you've made it clear what you need," he said over his shoulder. "Hold your horses, little girl."

"I am not a little girl," she muttered.

When the man returned, he took a pencil from behind his ear and scribbled on the back of a discarded ticket. "Here, kiddo. Circus folk stick together."

Effy took the scrap of paper and glanced at the name of the town. Satisfied, she thanked the man and hurried off. So, she was circus folk now. Poor Aunt Ada would be spinning in her grave.

Effy saved her pennies by walking to Union Railway Station. Her feet ached until she hardly noticed her throbbing head. Before she reached the railway building, she stepped inside the telegraph office wedged between the bank and the post office. Placing her precious coins on the marble counter, Effy dictated her message:

Phineas Rimaldi Stop Your daughter is arriving on the 8:00 PM train Stop Worry not Stop She has her own education trust fund Stop

Outside, Effy walked the final two blocks to the train station, her embroidered bag feeling heavier by the minute. She shifted its cloth handles from one hand to the other hand.

When she reached the ticket office, she purchased a

passage to Bridal Falls and stepped onto the train platform.

Once again, Effy didn't look back.

A train whistle shrieked, and the locomotive appeared in a cloud smelling of coal and oil. Wheels screamed against the metal tracks. As the train pulled to a stop, porters slammed stepping-platforms against the doors. The engine heaved steam like a panting black dragon, and the beast spat out its travellers.

Effy moved toward a door, muttering under her breath. "No need to scrutinize me, Mr. Conductor. Please don't stare at me, seedy-looking man loitering by the tracks." She hoped her face gleamed with confidence as she climbed the steps. She brushed away a porter's hand when he reached for her embroidered bag.

"Where do you suppose you're going all by yourself, young lady?" asked the conductor, who was directing passengers to their railway cars. He looked over his spectacles at her, then waggled his finger, directing her closer.

Effy held her breath when she stuck her ticket under the conductor's nose. He stared at it. In Effy's best imitation of her Aunt Ada's no-nonsense voice, she said, "I'm travelling to Bridal Falls, as you can clearly see."

The conductor frowned. "And who are you travelling with?" He looked over her shoulder.

"I am ... ah ... joining my party on the train." Effy hoped he didn't notice her white knuckles as she clutched the cloth handles of her bag.

"The rules are clear." The conductor shook his head slowly. "No unaccompanied children, little girl."

"I'm *not* a little girl, and I'm not travelling alone." *This isn't a lie*, she told herself. *There are loads of people on that train.* Effy held the conductor's gaze, but realized he wasn't convinced one whit. She turned toward the seedy-looking man leaning against the column. Waving at him, she shouted, "Hurry, Uncle, the train is leaving."

The man gazed back in surprise and stepped toward her. A bolt of terror travelled from Effy's heart to her toes. She hustled onto the train as the conductor shouted, "Come back this minute!"

Effy hid in the vestibule between the Pullman cars until the engine belched clouds of black smoke. The whistle shrilled as the carriage lurched and clattered along the tracks.

"I've made it." She let out a sigh as loud as a steaming kettle.

She then worked her way through the maze of people

sitting on the floor in the first passenger car. The wooden benches were packed with people jostling each other for seat space. The air reeked of sweat and onion and chicken feathers. Many folk balanced boxes on their laps, and inside one box, she definitely heard clucking.

There wasn't a spare inch of space in the next car, either. Effy kept moving. Finally in the third car, benches gave way to wooden seats. She spotted an empty chair and sat down with her bag on her lap. *I wonder why everyone jammed themselves into the first two railway cars. This is much nicer.*

The carriage door burst open, and the snoopy conductor strode down the aisle toward her. When he glanced up from his fistful of tickets, Effy grabbed her bag and hurried away, feeling his eyes bore into her back. She raced down the narrow aisle, through the vestibule, and into the next Pullman car. The swaying train unsettled her stomach.

Effy hoped it was her overactive imagination when she heard a door open and close behind her. Surely the conductor had better things to do than chase a paying passenger through the train. She darted into the next car.

She couldn't blame her imagination when she distinctly heard the slamming of the next car door. Lifting her skirt and petticoats, she dashed into a shiny, mahogany-panelled carriage. The seats were no longer wooden but upholstered. There were even footstools.

Effy spotted an empty seat across from a woman and a girl. She smiled as she sat down. Opening her embroidered bag, Effy pulled out her navy cloak. Even though it was stuffy inside the train, she slipped on her cloak and took off her hat.

When Effy heard the car door open, she quickly reached inside her bag, pulled out her dog-eared copy of *The Swiss Family Robinson*, and shoved the book in front of her face.

Effy hoped no one noticed that her book was shaking.

CHAPTER FOUR

A GOOD EDUCATION

"Is that a good book?"

The girl looked a bit older than Effy, and had blonde ringlets festooned with pink ribbons.

The conductor slowly made his way down the aisle. He was counting passengers on his fingers. The woman sitting beside the girl turned her head, adjusted her enormous hat covered in silk roses, and smiled at her daughter. Then she turned her gaze on Effy.

"I beg your pardon, but I asked if that was a good book?" The girl leaned closer. "I'm not much of a reader myself." She picked up the book beside her, titled *Black Beauty*. "But I just started this one. It's about horses."

Say something to the girl, Effy told herself. She managed, but it was a raspy whisper. "*The Swiss Family Robinson* is my favourite book."

"Is there a horse in it?" asked the girl.

"No," said Effy.

"What about a handsome prince?"

"No."

The conductor stopped beside them, and Effy buried her face deeper into the book.

"A damsel in distress, then?" the girl said.

"No." Sweat trickled down Effy's back. Her cloak was far too hot.

"Surely there's a girl who finds her one true love and lives happily ever after?" the girl asked expectantly. "Otherwise, it wouldn't be a very interesting story."

Effy could feel the conductor's stare burn through the pages.

"Well, is there?" asked the girl.

Effy inhaled sharply as the conductor cleared his throat in a loud, "harrumph." She couldn't stop her hands trembling. He finished counting, scowled, then moved on to the next Pullman car. Effy let out the breath she hadn't realized she'd been holding.

"Well?"

"Pardon me?" asked Effy.

The girl wore an amused smile. "Is there a happily-ever-after where the girl and boy marry in that Swiss Family book?"

"No. Well, yes. I mean, two people do get married,

but that isn't the main theme of the story." Effy was flustered. Acting carefree between heart-stopping moments wasn't easy.

The girl frowned. "It doesn't sound like a good book to me."

"There's a shipwreck!" Effy forced herself to concentrate. "And the family has lots of adventures, and they even fight off pirates."

"So, someone rescues the girl from pirates? That's not too bad, then." The girl eyed the book with more interest.

Effy decided not to mention that everyone rescued themselves. She lowered her book and slipped off her cloak. Then she finally relaxed into the seat's comfy upholstery.

"Is your mother joining us?" asked the girl.

Effy tried to think of what to say. Perhaps fib or be vague? The problem was, words usually burst from her mouth before her brain could measure their worth.

"Mother and I are returning from a dreadfully boring trip to a girls finishing school," said the girl in pink. She glared at her mother and said in a confiding voice, "There are no horse stables. All the girls in that school had to wear the ugliest navy smocked blouses and long skirts, like nuns. And there's not a boy for miles."

"Sofia," her mother said sharply.

Maybe Effy needn't worry about saying the wrong thing. She didn't have to say anything. Sofia had no problem single-handedly carrying on a conversation.

"I'm sorry, Mama, but I have no interest in learning how to create proper centrepieces for the dining table. Nor do I care a whit about the proper hat to wear."

"Oh, Sofia," the woman said with more exasperation than anger.

Effy couldn't resist discussing a girl's education. Her stopped-up words finally busted free. "I am going to an academic academy, and not one of those waste-of-time finishing schools."

Sofia's mother deepened her frown. Perhaps Effy shouldn't have mentioned that last point. She avoided eye contact and explained. "You see, I am in need of a broad education to discover my true purpose in life. I even have a good deal of money set aside for a college education equal to that of any man." She didn't add, *At least, I will have when I find my father, and he secures my trust fund.*

Sofia's eyes widened in surprise. "Don't be a goose; girls don't go to college."

"Sofia, you sound impertinent," the girl's mother pointed out.

Effy had heard a lot worse. She sighed. "It makes my blood boil that telegrams travel the world in minutes, and streetcars fly through streets at fifteen miles per hour, but people can't get it through their heads that girls should go to college." Those were Aunt Ada's words, but Effy had added one or two of her own.

The woman widened her eyes. "Those are bold thoughts."

"I'm sorry I called you a goose. For what it's worth, that's what I call all my friends." Sophia bit her lip. "I want to hear more."

The woman raised her eyebrows, then made a fuss of straightening her hat.

"Times are changing." Effy warmed to her favourite subject. "Why, there's a woman in New York who is an engineer. And Mrs. Emily Stowe and her daughter are doctors in Toronto. Soon women will enter any profession."

"And would girls attend those colleges with boys?" A slow smile spread across Sofia's face. Effy thought she may have missed the point.

"Excuse me, miss, but we didn't catch your name. Also, where is your mother?" The woman's voice had taken on a frostier tone.

Effy hesitated, realizing any more information than

her name was sure to get her into trouble.

The train carriage swayed along the tracks as Effy contemplated an answer. The last thing she needed was a whole slew of questions.

The woman reached out her gloved hand. "Forgive me. I should at least introduce myself first. I am Mrs. Winterbottom." Effy shook her hand.

"I'm Ephemia Rimaldi, but I prefer to be called Effy." Which, she realized, not a single person in her family had ever called her.

"Tell me more about these colleges, Effy." Sofia leaned forward.

Mrs. Winterbottom's eyebrows met in the middle of her forehead and formed a V when she said, "Did you say when your mother would join you?"

Effy aimed for an in-between nod of her head. Then she said, "The point isn't going to college with boys."

Sofia stuck out her bottom lip.

Effy pressed. "Women should study math and medicine, engineering and geography, and great literature, instead of which gloves and hats they should wear for spring."

Sofia shrugged. "Even so, I don't see the point of a profession if you're going to be a wife."

Thinking of her own problem, Effy felt it was also her duty to add, "What if your guardian passes to the Great Beyond. You'll need good accounting skills in case ... in case ..." Effy cleared her sticky throat. "... In case someone tries to cheat you."

A shadow crossed both Sofia's and Mrs. Winterbottom's faces. Mrs. Winterbottom daubed her eyes with a handkerchief. "You are quite right, young lady." She excused herself and hurried down the aisle.

Effy was sure that, once again, she'd misspoken. Only she didn't usually send a person fleeing. "Did I offend your mother?"

Sofia's eyes had turned glassy, but she shook her head. "My mother is a recent widow."

Effy placed her gloved hand to her lips. "Oh, I am so sorry. I, too, have suffered tragic loss." Whenever Effy thought of Aunt Ada, it was like a knife in her heart.

"My guardian, my dear aunt, recently departed. Now I'm rejoining my father, after a—long separation." Effy didn't add that she couldn't recall ever laying eyes on her poppa.

Sofia's face grew wistful. "Last summer, Father took me horseback riding. I was supposed to start riding lessons but ..." Sofia stumbled on those last words.

Even though Effy had no memories of a father's affection, she felt her throat ache. She patted Sofia's shoulder. "I'm so sorry. I can see how you miss him."

Sofia wiped away a tear and forced a smile. "As your father will have missed you, I'm sure. He will welcome his daughter with open arms." Her chin trembled. "Fathers love their little girls."

Mrs. Winterbottom returned. "Effy has also suffered loss, Mama," said Sofia. "She's being sent to live with her father."

Effy thought that was truthful enough. No need to mention she was the one doing the sending.

The conductor returned. "I beg your pardon, Madam, but there are too many passengers in this first-class car. May I see your tickets?" Mrs. Winterbottom reached into her drawstring bag and produced two tickets. Effy took her ticket and held it out.

"As I suspected! You are not with this party," the conductor said with satisfaction. "Not only are you an unaccompanied child ..." The way he shouted this was as if he was saying she was a common criminal. "... But this ticket is for third class." And the way the conductor said that, it was clear Effy had committed an even worse offence.

Effy's heart slammed against her ribs as she blurted,

"So, that's why people jammed themselves into the first two Pullman cars like chickens in a coop." Her face flushed. "I'm ... sorry, I didn't realize ..."

For a moment, Mrs. Winterbottom remained silent. Then her brown eyes softened. "We will make up the difference in the price of the ticket," she said, digging into her drawstring reticule. "Effy, do join us in the dining car as our guest."

"But the rules," the conductor sputtered. "Unaccompanied children are forbidden on this train."

Mrs. Winterbottom stood and adjusted her hat. "Stop bullying this girl. She is obviously with us now. Would you like me to take this up with the railway manager, as he is an acquaintance of mine?"

The conductor quickly apologized as his eyes shot daggers at Effy. Although it was most unladylike, she smirked back at him.

After the conductor left, Sofia offered Effy her hand. They made their way toward the dining car. When Sofia suddenly stopped, Effy banged into her.

"Look." Sofia bent over, picked up a glittering object, and held it out in her gloved hand. "If you find a hairpin, it means good luck." She pressed the pin into Effy's hand. "It means you'll make a new friend."

Hairpins, or pennies, for that matter, had never delivered her any luck. As a modern girl, Effy relied on reason in this scientific age. A hairpin couldn't predict anything.

Except, for once, she kept those words inside her mouth and smiled, and slipped the hairpin into her pocket instead.

As Effy supped on poached trout and drank sarsaparilla, neither Mrs. Winterbottom nor Sofia paid attention to Effy's unladylike appetite. She wolfed down everything but the linen tablecloth. As they sipped sweet-smelling tea from china cups, the sky pinked and then turned orange in the golden twilight.

By the time the train pulled into the platform at Bridal Falls, stars glittered in the night sky like sparklers against black satin. Effy reached for her bag and thanked Mrs. Winterbottom and Sofia for their pleasant company and delicious dinner.

Mrs. Winterbottom grabbed Effy's hand. "Not so fast, young lady." She said this smiling and without menace, but Effy's pulse still sped up.

Smoke belched from the train's chimney stack and added an extra layer of soot outside the window. Wheels screeched along the tracks as the locomotive pulled to a stop, its lurch knocking Effy against her chair. Mrs.

Winterbottom had yet to let go of her hand.

"Please introduce us to your father at the train platform," said Mrs. Winterbottom. "I want to caution him against purchasing third-class train tickets, which are quite unsuitable for an unaccompanied young lady."

"But ..."

"Worry not, I shan't scold the man." Mrs. Winterbottom added, "I'll be especially gentle on him because I wish to leave him my calling card."

"But ..."

"Goose," Sofia said kindly. "Mama and I want to invite you to tea."

The doors of the train yanked open. Porters shouted for the Bridal Falls passengers to please disembark. Outside the train window, Effy glanced at a few farmers getting down from their wagons, and buggy drivers circling beside the train platform. She didn't see anyone waiting for her.

It suddenly occurred to Effy that even though telegrams could send messages in seconds, there was no telling how long it would take for her telegram to be delivered to a travelling circus.

Mrs. Winterbottom and Sofia went searching for a porter to bring their trunks. Effy swallowed. She would have loved a friend. Only, Sofia and her mother didn't look like the sort of people who would approve of a poppa who was in the circus. Aunt Ada had called circus people riffraff.

Sighing, Effy slipped away. As she stepped from the train, she spotted the dratted conductor. He stood under a gas-lit lamp as if waiting for someone. She quickly stepped back into the shadows.

Effy could no longer deny the awful truth of it. She was a girl travelling alone, in the dark dead of night, while a meddlesome stickler waited for her. And until she found out where the circus had set up ...

... she had no place to go.

CHAPTER FIVE .

AN ARTFUL DODGE

The train station was only a dimly lit wooden structure with a roof and no walls. Beyond the station, Bridal Falls was an eerie black void. *There must be buildings and churches and houses with picket fences out there*, Effy said to herself. She just couldn't see them. When the conductor turned his back, Effy hurried across the platform.

Just as Effy stepped under the greenish glow of gaslight, he turned back. Before she could think of where to hide, the conductor rushed forward and grabbed her arm. Effy swallowed back a yelp.

"Rules are rules," said the conductor. "And you were an unaccompanied child on that train. I need to speak to your father. You are both in trouble."

Effy tugged her arm from the conductor's grasp. "Good sir, I beg your pardon." Effy tried imitating Mrs. Winterbottom. "I bid you to act more gentlemanly and leave me alone."

The conductor didn't bat an eye. "I'm not leaving until I've spoken to your father."

Effy couldn't tug her arm free. "Fine, my father is an important man and will happily discuss this with you. Of course," she warned, "he is also very protective of his little daughter." She blinked at him with wide eyes. "After all," she said, "*you* chased me on the train. You've left fingerprints on my dress sleeve." Effy pointed at the marks on her silk sleeve.

"I think that's dear Poppa climbing from his carriage now. Oh, my, he's carrying his carriage whip." Effy made a point of shuddering. "It surprises me how my father can turn into an angry brute when he hears I've been wronged."

The conductor released her arm and took a step back.

"And the fact that he's already slapping the whip against his leg is never a good sign." Effy tut-tutted. "I expect he's in one of his dark moods."

A train whistle shrieked, and the conductor quickly said, "Good evening, then." He scurried off the platform and onto the train.

Effy stared into the inky darkness as she calculated her next move. A small flurry of passengers crossed the platform and climbed onto waiting wagons. One horse-driven buggy was already leaving.

That's what I must do, thought Effy. *Follow the buggy driver's lantern as he lights up the path.* As the train chugged and belched steam along the tracks, Effy rushed after the buggy. She began humming a cheerful marching tune, almost hearing her dear Aunt Ada saying, "Onward and upward, Ephemia. The wind is at your back."

Effy set out from the station at a brisk pace, but in less than a few minutes, the horse-driven buggy had pulled so far ahead, she could no longer follow its tiny pinprick of light. Behind her, other carts and wagons followed. A carriage passed close enough to knock the hat from her head. She left the dirt road and made her way across a field smelling of dark, earthy loam and dry grass. Secret things chittered at the swish of her skirts.

A muffled roar broke across the tall grass, and she thought of bears or cougars. Tugging up her dress, Effy broke into a run. Scrambling blindly through the field, Effy knew there was no point running around like a chicken, waiting to launch herself into the jaws of a wild animal. Effy need a plan. Trees loomed ahead in the shadows.

When she needed a quiet space to think, she used to climb the huge oak tree on her great-aunt's property. Spotting a huge oak that forked into three trunks in the middle, she ran toward it. Effy slung her bag over her shoulder and scrambled up the tree with ease. She nestled between the other trunks, where a series of lower branches and leaves formed a nest.

Effy leaned against the largest trunk and placed her bag on her lap. She opened the bag, pulled out her cloak, and spread it over her arms and legs. After a time, Effy was convinced dawn had to be around the corner, but when she looked at the inky sky, the moon hadn't budged on the horizon.

Effy clutched the bag tighter. The last place she expected to be a week ago was perched up in a tree for the night like a great awkward bird. Surely this was all a dream.

"Don't hide your head in the sand, Ephemia. Face your problems."

Aunt Ada's words carried in the breeze. Fine, this was no dream, and it was going to be a long night. Twigs pressed against Effy's neck, bark bit into her back, but after a time, she became so exhausted, she hardly noticed. Under the warm weight of her cloak, her eyelids drooped. Effy jerked her head. No good would come from falling asleep in a tree—which is why she was surprised when she woke at first sunlight and found herself perched high above a pond. Effy threw down her bag and cloak, and then scrambled down from the oak tree.

She smoothed the deep wrinkles in her dress, and plucked out leaves and a couple of beetles from her hem. She looked up at the branches high above her head and felt a tremor in her heart. This could have ended badly.

Effy shrugged. She walked a few steps to the pond and splashed water on her face. Her unruly hair had become unbound, and she rewound it into a braid. Digging out the hairpin Sofia had found, Effy pinned the braid and put on her hat.

Now she was presentable. It was time to meet her poppa.

In the dark, she'd been concerned with escaping bears and cougars. She'd paid no attention to where she was going. Effy sighed and climbed back up the tree. Ahead, she spotted a cropping of rocks high on an escarpment. Twin waterfalls trailed down the cliffs, water spreading like two wedding veils. Effy smiled—Bridal Falls.

In the opposite direction, Effy spotted a huge field near the train platform. Further down a road, two-story buildings and houses dotted a main street. At the far end of the street, a field and brightly coloured caravans and half-raised canvases spread over the ground. She wondered if those dangerous sounds she'd heard in the night were circus animals.

After Effy climbed back down, she set out along the winding dirt road. A wagon lumbered by in a cloud of dust. She jumped out of the way until it passed. Grit coated her face. Stumbling on a rock, Effy fell and tore the edge of her silk skirt. Scrapes scuffed her fine leather boots. She wished she had Aunt Ada's new-fangled bicycle that she'd secretly ridden in the carriage shed. Aunt Ada had called it a velocipede, and said it was a dangerous contraption. Despite scraped knees and bruised elbows, Effy had found it a lot of fun.

Limping slightly, Effy shouldered her bag. The sun rose over a canopy of yellow-leafed poplar trees. She paused and wiped a few beads of sweat under the brim of her straw boater's hat.

A swarm of midges followed her, and she had to keep swatting them away from her eyes. Her stomach grumbled. She passed two boys on the road. One boy walked alongside the other boy, who was running on top of a turning barrel.

"Say, you've taken the wrong fork in the road," said the boy on the road. He eyed Effy's embroidered bag and her dressy outfit. "You need to take the other road to the train platform. This road leads to Farmer Macleod's field, where they're setting up the circus."

"Thank you, but I'm heading in the right direction," said Effy. She kept walking, even though her toes ached.

"Do you think she's joining the circus?" said the barrel rider. "She's carrying a bag like she's run off."

"Nah," scoffed his friend. "She's a girl. What can a girl do in a circus?"

"Anything a boy can," Effy snapped back. Not that she had *any* interest in joining the circus. She simply needed her poppa to sort out her trust fund, and she'd be off to the academy.

Effy crossed the sawdust-strewn grounds toward the circus wagons and men setting up striped tents. She licked her parched lips and tried ignoring the hunger pains in her stomach. It didn't work.

Her thoughts turned toward her poppa. She had no recollection at all of her mother or father, nor had she ever seen a tintype picture of them. Effy felt she resembled her mother's side, because she had a similar nose and chin to her farm cousins. While most of the Rimaldis she knew had grey hair, she must have gotten her dark hair and green eyes from their side.

Effy stopped. Would she even recognize her poppa?

"Onward and upward," she repeated. "The wind is at your back." Except that wasn't true. There was no wind at all, not a puff, and sweat dribbled and pooled under her armpits.

Men grunted lifting heavy poles, and horses snorted, hauling even heavier beams. Effy elbowed her way through a group of gawking farm boys who'd gathered at the edge of the circus grounds. She distinctly heard the roar of a large cat. Not a cougar, she decided, but a lion or tiger. Oh, my.

"Are you lost, dearie?" a kindly voice said behind her. "Surely that bag you're clutching isn't because you've run off to join a circus. You hardly seem the type."

Effy spun around and gasped. *"Compose yourself,"* she imagined Aunt Ada saying. *"A young woman shows good deportment, no matter what the situation."*

She wondered if Aunt Ada had ever found herself in the situation of meeting face-to-face with a bearded lady.

CHAPTER SIX

A COMMITTEE OF VULTURES

"I ... um, I'm here to ..." Effy gathered her wits. "I'm here to see Phineas Rimaldi."

"Do tell," the bearded woman said, with a wink. "You're not a bill collector, are you? If so, you'll have to take your place in line. The ringmaster is very busy."

"I'm not a bill collector."

The woman chuckled. "I know that, dearie, I was making a joke. Now run along. He's a busy man."

"He will be most interested in meeting me."

"The ringmaster? Now, surely *you* joke." The bearded lady took her time checking Effy over, from the wilting strands of hair that had escaped her straw hat to her scuffed leather boots.

"Once again, please summon Phineas Rimaldi." Aunt Ada had always told Effy, *"If you mean business, you must look a person in the eye,"* and Effy was doing her best. But it was near impossible not to let her gaze slide down the shiny chestnut waves of beard that fell past the woman's ample chest.

Another woman strode over. "Is something going on, Miss Mabel?"

Miss Mabel, the bearded lady, nodded, but instead of explaining, she said, "Young lady, Phineas Rimaldi is not what you'd call an even-tempered man. You'd be best not bothering him."

The second woman was dressed in a star-patterned silk robe and wearing a turban. Meeting Effy's curious gaze, she said with a more exotic accent, "I am Madame Vadoma, za circus mystic. Forget Phineas for now. You'd best let me tell your fortune first. Do you have ze nickel?"

Effy shook her head, then turned sharply toward the tallest man she had ever seen, walking alongside the tiniest woman she had ever seen. They drew closer. Not far away, a creature made a trumpeting sound, and a wild cat roared in response.

Effy had landed in a whole other world.

"What's going on?" A wiry man stopped beside them. His muscles strained from the pole he carried over his stooped shoulders, and he seemed more than happy to drop it. The pole bounced, stirring up small tornadoes of sawdust.

"Cat's got her tongue now," said Miss Mabel, "but she claims Phineas will be interested in her."

The others gaped. Effy squared her shoulders. "I demand to speak with Phineas Rimaldi. It is urgent."

The man wiped his forehead with a grimy scarf. Then he grinned and said, "I'll get him. This should be interesting."

Effy stared straight ahead as more people gathered around her. Never before had Effy even seen such a medley of folk. Then a girl not much older than Effy waltzed up, wearing only her underthings. Effy felt her cheeks blush. Then her face heated even more when an older boy appeared, wearing a similar skimpy outfit.

They both gave Effy a scornful glance, and the boy muttered, "Who is this hoity-toity girl?"

A man in giant floppy shoes joined them. Yet Effy was the centre of *their* attention. She didn't care for it. The last thing she needed was an audience when she first laid her eyes on her poppa. It needed to be a private moment.

"Who is *demanding* to see me?" A silver-haired man with a short beard and a moustache waxed into pointy tips strode toward them. The tails of his long red coat flapped in his wake. He didn't look a bit like a proper poppa—or at least, the one that Effy had imagined, with a pocket watch tucked in a paisley vest, and side whiskers on his kindly face.

Goodness, thought Effy. *He looks like Buffalo Bill from the Wild West posters.* He was accompanied by a burly man in a black captain's hat. Effy swallowed the dust in her mouth.

"What in tarnation is the problem here? I have a circus to set up." As Phineas Rimaldi stood in the clearing, he glared at the group who had gathered around Effy. "Don't you all have jobs to do?"

They began backing away, but stopped when the ring-master spotted Effy. He scowled. "Not another runaway."

He turned to the man in the captain's cap and shouted, "I've told you, Jefferson, I'm not a collector of strays. You're the boss-handler, and you should have handled this."

Phineas faced Effy. "Go home, child. You're too young to join the circus."

"Actually, joining the circus is the last thing I'd ever want to do," Effy snapped. "I'm the girl most likely to run *away* from the circus."

"Thinks she's too good for us, does she?" The boy in the underwear glared at her. "I knew it."

"She does look like a prissy thing," the girl said.

"I most certainly do not," Effy said, and quickly realized her words did sound a bit prissy.

Madam Vadoma took in Effy's fine boots and silk dress. "Well, I'm curious. What on earth is a girl like you doing here in the first place?"

Some fortune teller, Effy thought.

"My guess is this girl has a bone to pick," said the little woman, whose eyes seemed to miss nothing.

"I agree, Miss Dot. That child's got some grit in her, even if she is a little girl," said Miss Mabel. "You've got to admit that."

"I'm not a little girl," Effy shot back.

"Told yeh," said Miss Mabel.

Phineas held up his hand to silence the others. He stared at Effy until she squirmed under his scrutiny. Why had Effy gone and told him she didn't like circuses? She'd never even attended one. Instead of polite introductions, she'd sounded like a hissing cat.

"You would run *away* from a circus, eh?" said Phineas. "Well, then, we're agreed." He turned to the boss-handler and growled, "Send her home, and all of you get back to work." He began walking away.

"Only ... I have no other place to go—Poppa."

The others gasped in one short burst. Phineas spun

around as Effy clutched the handles of her embroidered bag so tightly, her fingers turned white.

He opened his mouth and closed it several times.

More circus folk gathered, and whispers rose in a shudder as if a flock of birds had flown overhead.

"Last warning—get back to work!" Phineas bellowed. Except for Mr. Jefferson, Miss Mabel, and Madam Vadoma, they scrambled away.

He took two long strides, until he loomed over Effy. In a low, yet most unsettling voice, he said, "What did you just say?"

Effy took a step backward. She swallowed and then blurted, "I am Ephemia, your daughter. And I need my legal guardian if I want to protect my education trust."

Once the words were out of her mouth, Effy wondered if she should have introduced herself with more endearments, such as, "I've longed to be with you all my days, Poppa," or "Have you missed your little girl? She's missed you."

Only those words would have been lies. She'd been told countless times that Phineas Rimaldi was a scoundrel who'd abandoned her. She wouldn't pretend any love was lost between them.

"I won't cost you a penny, but I need your help to

get my trust fund and return to the academy. And then attend college," Effy added.

Phineas, who did not seem like anyone's poppa, simply held Effy in his gaze until she added, "Otherwise, a committee of Rimaldi vultures will swoop in and leave me penniless."

"Rimaldi vultures." Phineas chuckled. "Well, you're right about that. Perhaps we're related, after all."

"So, you will help me," Effy declared.

"Yes," said Phineas. "Back onto the train."

CHAPTER SEVEN
SPIT AND VINEGAR

A few of the circus folk had regrouped and shuffled forward, clinging to the tent shadows behind Phineas. They gawped at Effy. Her stomach fluttered as she thought, *Step right up folks, the show's about to begin.*

"You're sending me back on the train? You can't." Now it was Effy's turn to open and close her mouth.

"Yes, I can," said Phineas. "Back into the arms of Ada, that bossy old biddy. I know she's no easy woman to deal with, but you're her concern now. She can hold those other vultures off."

Effy's blood boiled. She stood on her toes and stretched until the top of her head reached his shoulders. She looked up and shouted, "How dare you call Aunt Ada an old biddy? She was teaching me to search for my true purpose. For that, I'll need a college education. *And for that,* I'm forced to request your assistance."

"Was?"

"Aunt Ada has passed to the Great Beyond." Effy fought to keep the tremor out of her voice.

"Telegram, I've a telegram for one Phineas Rimaldi." A young man on a horse raced across the circus grounds. Phineas stretched out his arm and took the message.

"It's customary to provide a tip, sir," the boy said.

Phineas ignored him as he tore open the telegram. After he read it, he scowled at Effy. "You arrived last night? Where did you sleep?"

"In a tree." Effy shrugged.

"Perhaps a free admission to the circus for my tip?" suggested the messenger boy.

"Leave us be," bellowed Phineas, and the boy took off as if a circus tiger was chasing him. Phineas crumpled the telegram. Only Madam Vadoma and the bearded lady, Miss Mabel, hovered close by.

"You foolish child," Phineas said gruffly. "Go back to your proper home. When there's time, I'll look into this."

Effy would not let him get the best of her. The awful truth was, this man, her so-called poppa, didn't care a fig about her and wanted her out of his hair. She dug in her heels. "Phineas, you left me wailing in the arms of a family that cared nothing for me. My mother's people hated me ... and you!"

A winter's frost spread over Phineas's face. "Your mother wanted a different life than farming. I would have given her anything and everything."

The way Phineas said those last words, as if each one was a knife stabbing into him, made Effy realize she'd gone too far. And if it wasn't rage that glazed his eyes, it was close.

"I see now. Like her kin, you also hold my mother's death against me." Effie swallowed several times until she could say evenly, "I was a baby and had no choice to be born. It wasn't my fault *we* lost her."

"No, it was not." Phineas held her gaze. Then he said more quietly, "Yet she is gone, and I am no father, and you *are no circus performer*."

Phineas turned away. "I will see to it you are put safely on the train."

The circus was where she needed to be. "Do you wish to see your own flesh and blood turned into a hired girl working in a ... a boarding house?"

Phineas kept walking. "Your dear Aunt Ada would find working in a boarding house far more respectable than living in a circus. I told you: I'll look into things when I have time."

Time was what the other Rimaldis needed to bribe a judge and take away her trust fund. Effy gathered her shredding courage. "If you don't care about me, what do you suppose the woman you loved so much would think of you abandoning me again? After all, that woman was my mother."

Phineas spun around so fiercely—Effy thought he might drill himself into the ground. Thunder clouds hooded his eyes. It no longer mattered that Effy clutched her bag to keep her hands steady. Her whole body trembled. As Phineas lurched forward, she refused to step back this time.

"I never abandoned you. I was not fit to raise an infant. I left you in the hands of people who could." Phineas gave a short bow. "Good day, girl." Then he turned and stormed away, leaving Effy in his dust.

"It's not 'girl'—it's 'daughter,'" Effy said.

Miss Mabel said, "He's a busy man; pay him no mind."

Madam Vadoma whispered, "He's like that with everyone."

Effy dropped her head and stared at her scuffed boots. For a few moments, she pretended they were the most interesting boots in the world. While Effy had prepared herself for what her father was—a scoundrel—she'd made no plan for what he wasn't. The awful truth: Phineas Rimaldi was no father.

Madam Vadoma raced after the ringmaster. They bowed their heads and exchanged words, sharp and fast, as if two snakes were having a conversation.

"Dearie, you look like you'll take a tumble right here on the spot. Why don't we get some food into you," said Miss Mabel, who, despite her bearded strangeness, struck Effy as kind. "Come with me to the food tent."

Miss Mabel tucked Effy under her arm, and Effy felt herself pressed against Miss Mabel's soft body. She guided her behind the circus caravans where they stopped by the cook wagon. The smell of beans and molasses almost made Effy pass out with hunger. Miss Mabel led her over to a bench and Effy sat with a thump, entirely unsure if she'd be able to get up again. Those legs of hers were proving untrustworthy. *Imagine your spine is strung with steel,"* she heard Aunt Ada saying. *"Pull yourself up and get on with things."*

Effy would do that, only perhaps not at this moment.

Miss Mabel went behind the wagon, and when she returned, she was followed by a barrel of a man wearing a stained apron.

"I don't see much of a resemblance," harrumphed the man.

"You'd recognize her spit and vinegar," said Miss Mabel.

"*I* have no doubt." She handed Effy a tin cup filled with apple cider and a tin plate of steaming beans.

Effy downed the crisp cider in two gulps and when Miss Mabel went to refill her cup, she laid into those beans as if it was a Christmas turkey feast. The sweet smoky tang of the molasses filled her mouth.

"Thank you, this is delicious," Effy said to the man in the apron, between mouthfuls.

"Don't usually get compliments," muttered the man. "Lately, it's always, 'why is there no meat?' or 'yer cornbread is stale.'" He walked away with a smile.

As Effy sipped her second cup of cider, Madam Vadoma returned.

"So, what has that ornery buzzard decided, Vadoma?" asked Miss Mabel.

Instead of answering, Madam Vadoma said to Effy, "Phineas will allow you to stay, temporarily."

Effy let out a sigh of relief. Temporarily was all she needed. She clung to the fact that Phineas had not cut all ties with her. He was still her legal guardian. All Effy needed was to remain in his view until he remembered his fatherly duty.

"I knew it." Miss Mabel smiled at Effy. "Vadoma always finds a way to soften his gizzard."

"But you must work here like everyone else," cautioned Madam Vadoma. "Phineas won't abide a pampered guest."

Work—in a circus! Would Aunt Ada get no chance to rest in peace? "No disrespect, Madam Vadoma, but I am not the circus type."

Madam Vadoma frowned. "And what type might that be?"

Effy didn't offer Aunt Ada's opinion: scalawags and riffraff types.

"Best not to cross the ringmaster, so we'll find something for you to do until then," said Miss Mabel. She stared at Effy's fine silk dress. "Though, I'm sorely pressed as to what."

"Perhaps you can assist me," said Madam Vadoma. "The circus doesn't open until tomorrow, but I'm expecting an important customer this afternoon." She eyed Effy in a most calculating way.

"Do you have clothes that would draw less... attention? Something plain and dour?" asked Madam Vadoma.

"I have my black funeral dress."

"Yes, that vill be perfect." Madam Vadoma's accent had thickened again. "Perfect for the spirit I vill be channelling."

What twaddle, Effy thought, but didn't say.

CHAPTER EIGHT

THE FLIMFLAM LIFE

Effy followed Madam Vadoma to the other side of the midway, where colourful caravans stood in several rows. Next to the half-raised big top, they stopped at the first caravan. Painted on its side were crescent moons and stars, and the word *Mystic*.

"My wagon is closest to the midway," said Madam Vadoma, whose accent had, once more, evaporated. "So I can help customers before and after the show."

"Help them? With what?"

"With easing their hearts," said Madam Vadoma. "They come to me so I can contact their departed loved ones about unfinished business. If you want, I could try and contact your departed Aunt ..."

"No, thank you," Effy said. "Just tell me what *I'm* here for."

She was trying to be polite. After all, this woman had convinced that scoundrel, Phineas, to let her stay. It was

Effy's duty to show gratitude, even though she wanted no part in flimflamming innocent people.

Madam Vadoma climbed two wooden steps and opened the door to her caravan. Heavy incense filled the air. She invited Effy to join her within its murky depths. Veils embroidered with silver stars draped the walls and hung from the ceiling. In the middle of the caravan stood a small table and two chairs, and a crystal ball sat on the table.

"Change into your black dress first," ordered Madam Vadoma. "Then you can help me set up my séance. Once the customer arrives at the ticket booth, we'll let her wait for a bit."

Madam Vadoma winked. "People appreciate my services more if they're left to anticipate for a while."

Not if Aunt Ada had been her customer, Effy thought. She had never been partial to slow service.

"You will then lead the customer in here." Madam Vadoma busied herself checking cords tucked under the Turkish carpet, and pulling almost invisible strings dangling from hung veils.

"You appear to be a clever girl, so feed me any useful information you hear from the customer," said Madam Vadoma. "Then I can read her better."

Effy tried once again to like this woman. "I'm ... not sure this is the right job for me."

"I'm not actually giving you a choice," Madam Vadoma said firmly.

"Very well, then perhaps you could direct me to where I could bathe before I change into my dress," said Effy, trying to delay the inevitable. "I've had a long and dusty walk to the circus."

Madam Vadoma sighed. "Follow me." She led Effy to the back of the last caravan. Behind it, a couple of sheets had been draped over the low-hanging branches of a gold-leafed maple tree. Madam Vadoma stopped at a pump at the bucket station and filled two buckets with water. Handing one bucket to Effy, she led her behind the sheets and set the second bucket on the ground.

"One bucket is to wash; one bucket is to rinse. Not a drop more." Madam Vadoma left as Effy stared at the buckets in horror.

Effy blushed, thinking about taking off her dress when the only thing separating her from the hustle bustle of the circus was a flimsy bed sheet. She'd bathed in the kitchen in a tin tub, back on the farm, but then she'd been a little girl. Aunt Ada's home had proper facilities, including a claw-footed bathtub. She stared at the buckets.

"Well, are you going to wash, or what?" The girl in the long underwear burst through the sheets and set down her own buckets. "I'll be glad when the autumn coolness arrives. I hate this grimy heat when I'm swinging on the trapeze."

Effy quickly turned her back as the girl shrugged out of her tights and shirt.

"Aren't you the delicate pearl," the girl scoffed.

Circus life will never be for me, Effy thought. Phineas would simply have to listen. She needed him to straighten out her finances with the family immediately. Abandoning her buckets, she carefully ducked under the sheet to protect the other girl's modesty. Not that the girl seemed to care as she shouted, "If you aren't using those buckets, I will." Water splashed.

Effy hurried along the caravans in search of Phineas. Some caravans were painted green or red or purple, but one caravan, at the outermost edge of the field had a cherry-red door. The wagon was gilded with an elephant painted on the side. Above the mural, letters scrolled: The Rimaldi Circus. That caravan had to be the ringmaster's. Effy crossed between narrow rows of wagons, but as she stepped out from the caravan next to the ringmaster's, she quickly stepped back into the shadows. An argument was going on.

An old man and a boy stood at the steps of Phineas's wagon. Phineas leaned from his door shouting, "That creature of yours is eating up all my profit!"

"Elephants have to eat," the boy shouted back. "What do you expect?"

"I expect not to go broke," Phineas barked. "Make sure you improve your act, so we sell more tickets, or that beast is going to be auctioned off." Phineas went back inside, slamming the red door behind him.

"You can't do that to her," the boy begged through the door. "Or you will sentence Balally to a terrible fate. She deserves better."

"It is no use, nephew," said the old man as he turned to leave. "One elephant is not enough of an attraction anymore. I hear in Chicago, there's a circus with three rings and twenty elephants. They all line up and dance on their feet in ballet tutus."

The boy let out a disgusted grunt. "Uncle, my Balally is not about to dance for anyone. It is not dignified."

"Your Balally, is it?" The uncle chuckled. "So, when did I promote you from being my water-boy?"

"You know I am more to Balally than just her water-boy."

"I fear she is too old to go to another circus." The

uncle waited until other workers hustled past. Then he said, "Everything, including circuses, is going modern. Our days here are numbered."

Effy shouldn't spy. But what was going to happen to them, and why wouldn't Phineas help?

"We must return Balally to an elephant sanctuary in Ceylon," said the boy.

The uncle sighed. "That requires money."

"We must sell our sapphire." The boy slammed his fists together.

"You know that gem is cursed," the uncle said.

"But Uncle, how can we be sure it is truly cursed?" said the boy. Effy quietly agreed.

"I've tried to sell the sapphire before. Once, robbers heard I was trying to sell it, and we had to flee our village. Remember the second time, the buyer was poisoned. My cousin was forced to share the inheritance, so he gave me a cursed sapphire in trickery."

Relatives and inheritance seemed a wicked business, thought Effy.

The uncle shook his head. "We must choose very carefully what to do with that sapphire. We ourselves have proven it brings bad luck to any man who tries to profit from it."

The boy spoke softly, sadly, but Effy moved away, even though she still burned with curiosity. Phineas appeared to be in a sour mood. Perhaps it wasn't the best time to call on him. Instead, Effy hurried back to the bucket station where she pumped a thin stream of water, just enough to rinse her hands and face.

When she returned to Madam Vadoma's wagon, the so-called mystic was waiting for her on the steps. "What took you so long?"

Effy shrugged into her dress, no pleasant task when her skin was sticky, and the back of her neck itched miserably under her starched collar. She scurried to the ticket booth. An older woman, also dressed in funeral black, waited in the shade and kept sighing heavily. She opened and shut a locket that hung around her neck and stared at the tiny portrait, saying, "How I miss you."

Effy led the woman to the caravan and, as the mystic had ordered, asked her to wait a few moments. The woman once again took out her locket. Effy entered the caravan, stepping into the cloying scent of myrrh. She said in a flat voice, "You have a widow who I believe is in need of comforting words about her recently departed husband."

Madam Vadoma smiled. "Well done."

Effie sighed. "You're asking me to trick a lonely

widow. You're not asking me to calculate engineering equations like Emily Roebling."

"Are you always like this?" Madam Vadoma frowned.

Effy stared. "What do you mean?"

"You act superior, as if much is beneath you." The mystic's frown deepened into a scowl.

"I most certainly do not," Effy scoffed. Which did sound superior, she supposed. What *was* the truth of it? "I ... just don't think you should cheat people out ... of ..." Madam Vadoma put her hand up cutting her off.

"It's challenging work finding comforting words to ease a grieving person's heart," said Madam Vadoma. "I rely on intuition—and I, and many others, believe I channel those thoughts from the next plane, the Great Beyond."

Effy managed to bite back her opinion.

"Maybe using my gift is not as challenging as being the woman in charge of building the Brooklyn Bridge, but it is difficult enough," snapped Madam Vadoma. "Now please bring in my customer. And when she arrives, I need you to make tapping sounds against the wall with your boot heel."

Effy's jaw dropped.

Madam Vadoma wagged her finger below Effy's nose. "If I want to help the widow, she must be sure I've summoned her departed husband. The thumping is for extra effect."

Only when Effy led the woman inside the caravan, did it occur to her that Madam Vadoma knew all about Emily Roebling, the engineer for the Brooklyn Bridge. She brooded on that as the customer sat across from the mystic.

"I see the ethereal mists gathering," said Madam Vadoma in an eerie, distant voice. She swayed back and forth and stared into her crystal ball.

The whole crystal ball appeared cloudy to Effy.

Madam Vadoma swayed harder. Effy had to admit the effect was uncanny, particularly as Madam Vadoma had draped a veil over her entire head.

In the murky light inside the caravan, Effy barely saw the subtle twist of Madam Vadoma's wrist as she pulled an invisible string. The woman gasped as the tablecloth swished around its edges. Then one end of the table rose off the ground.

"I hear him," Madam Vadoma told the widow in her drifty voice. Her veiled head bobbed as if it was also attached to strings.

"He ... he haz an important message vor youuuuu ..." her voice faded and then got louder as she wobbled back and forth in her chair. Madam Vadoma paused, waiting for Effy to tap her boot. "I *said* he has an important message for you."

Effy couldn't listen a moment longer while Madam Vadoma pumped twaddle and confabulation into her customer's ears.

"He's telling you not to use your money trying to contact him," Effy shouted.

The woman looked up with a startled expression. Then she sniffed. "Why, that's exactly what Horace would say. Thank you."

After the woman left, Madam Vadoma marched Effy back to the cook wagon. Effy tried explaining. "I didn't mean to ruin your business, but it's wrong to take advantage of widows and the poor and ..."

Madam Vadoma deposited Effy on the bench, saying to Mabel, "It's your turn. I have no use for this girl."

CHAPTER NINE

THE DARING YOUNG GIRL ON THE FLYING TRAPEZE

"I'm not sure *what* to do with you," Miss Mabel said after Madam Vadoma left. She grabbed a giant wooden spoon and began stirring a cauldron of beans on the camp stove.

Cook threw in a handful of fresh-picked greens, and Miss Mabel batted him away. "No more dandelion leaves; it will make the sauce bitter."

"When I lived on the farm, I peeled lots of vegetables *and* dug them up. I could help out here." Effy held out strong fingers.

The cook placed a big mixing bowl on a wobbly stool next to the camp stove and poured in a sack of cornmeal. He cracked eggs and tossed them into the bowl. When he crooked his arm and began mixing, Miss Mabel dodged his elbow. She sighed heavily. "As you can see, two cooks in this tent are one cook too many." The cook raised his bushy eyebrows but nodded in agreement.

"I ran my Aunt Ada's printing press, turning out

hundreds of leaflets on women's rights. Turning those press handles was hard work." Effy flexed her arm and pointed to a muscle.

"Well, then, perhaps you should go see Mr. Jefferson." Mabel put her hands on her hips. "The boss-handler is a smart man who can find a fit for anyone in the circus. There's nothing he can't figure out."

Miss Mabel said that last bit with a heartfelt sigh, and when she looked at Effy's smile, she blushed. "Off with you, then. Phineas doesn't tolerate idleness."

Effy found the burly boss-handler supervising workers as they raised the giant canvas for the big top. Men were pounding more poles into the ground. The air was heavy with the smell of canvas and the sharp stink of kerosene that coated the outside layer to keep out the rain. Effy had heard of terrible tragedies in circuses when canvases caught on fire. This tent had four exits in case of disaster.

"Mr. Jefferson, sir, may I be of service to you?" she asked the man in the captain's hat.

The boss-handler raised his bushy black eyebrows. "Having a hard time fitting in here, are you?" He chuckled.

Effy bristled. "I can do a lot of things, such as ..." she stared at the folded canvas and shrugged, "tying ropes. I can tie double hitches."

"We could use a hand securing this pole," said a tall, thin boy. He pointed at high scaffolding where a rope ladder dangled twenty feet from the top. "I can't climb that rope without swinging around, and I hate goin' under ladders. It's terrible bad luck, and this circus has had plenty of that already."

Mr. Jefferson scowled. "I'll tell you what would be bad luck, Willy. If this girl falls like Humpty Dumpty and cracks her skull. Not to mention, Phineas will eat you for breakfast, and then chew me up for supper."

"I doubt he gives a fig," Effy said quietly.

The boss-handler gave her a thoughtful look.

"I used to climb the knotted rope that hung from the tallest tree on the farm," said Effy. "I know a trick that will keep the ladder from swinging." Effy hoped she'd be able to raise her arms high enough in her stiffly starched dress. She looked down at her boots and debated whether she should climb the rope in her bare feet. No, the heel would give her purchase. She lifted her skirts above her ankle and approached the ladder.

"When you climb, you use your hands to hold and balance your weight, and then push up with your legs." Effy grabbed the first rope rung and quickly climbed the next six.

"You're awful fine at climbing, Miss. Why don't you keep going and secure the pole?" said Willy, looking hopeful.

"Hold on, now." The boss-handler gently grasped Effy's waist and tugged her back to the ground. "Thank you, Miss Ephemia, he gets the picture."

Mr. Jefferson jabbed a finger under Willy's nose. "Get to work."

"Now I have to prove to myself I can climb the ladder," grumbled Willy. "Can't let no girl show me up."

"Then you'll have a real problem." Mr. Jefferson laughed. "In the circus, girls and ladies swing from trapezes and walk across tight ropes, same as boys and men. What will you do about that?"

Willy said nothing. He was too busy grasping the ladder rungs until his knuckles were white as his face. He let out a soft whimper as the ladder swung back and forth. Effy felt a smidge of pity. It was a long way to the top.

"You have to keep a firm grip on the next rung before you slide your feet off," she said, "and keep your weight in the centre. That stops the rope from twisting around."

"Sounds about right, I s'pose." Willy held tightly and stepped onto the next rung of the ladder.

Effy whispered to Mr. Jefferson. "I think he's really scared."

Jefferson grabbed the ladder and steadied it. "He'll be fine."

"If girls and ladies do the same work here as men, why won't you let me help?" asked Effy.

Mr. Jefferson placed one hand on Effy's shoulder and steered her back onto the midway. "Because—you're the ringmaster's daughter."

Effy sighed. "Miss Mabel told me you'd find a fit for me here, that you found a fit for everyone."

"Did she, then," Jefferson chuckled. A wistful smile softened his grizzled face. "She's a fine lady whom I wouldn't want to disappoint. But I just don't have the time to ponder. You'll find work if you keep asking."

Effy strode through the circus grounds. But every time she approached someone, she was shooed away by a worker too busy to give her the time of day. She came to a crossroads between the midway and the caravans. Two makeshift trapeze swings rigged from poles swung about six feet above, and a tightrope stretched between two pegs was suspended close to the ground.

The boy who'd been wearing underwear when she'd first met up with Phineas was now dressed in a plaid shirt and trousers. He idly crossed the tightrope back and forth with his arms outstretched. The girl who had taken Effy's water buckets had changed into a proper dress instead of tights. She swung back and forth on the low-rigged trapeze and stared sullenly at Effy.

Sitting on the caravan's step, a woman with her arm in a sling eyed Effy. "And who is this, Jacque?" asked the woman.

"She's none other than Miss Hoity-toity, the ringmaster's daughter." The boy spat on the ground when he jumped off the tightrope and glared at Effy.

"I can't help it if I'm the ringmaster's daughter." Effy put her hands on her hips.

"Where are your manners," the woman cautioned the boy, although, to Effy's mind, not overly so. "I am Yolanda, and that's Jacque and Madelene," she gestured to her children, "of the Great Yolandas. What can I do for you?"

Effy glanced at the woman's sling. "Perhaps you could use some extra help?"

"You want to be a trapeze artist?" Jacque laughed, and Madelene quickly joined in. It was as if he'd said the most hilarious thing in the world.

A trapeze artist—Effy's jaw dropped. Hanging upside down, on a swing, way up in the air, wasn't what she had in mind at all. She'd much rather climb rope ladders and tie poles. She was about to say so when Jacque snorted,

"She's no circus performer."

Effy was tired of people telling her what she wasn't. She decided there on the spot, whatever those two ruffians could do, she could learn. "Of course, I'm a performer. I'm the ringmaster's daughter. I can climb and jump. I used to jump off the barn roof all the time and fall onto the haystacks. And I have strong hands," she pointed out.

Madelene stopped swinging. "You are injured, Mama."

"No," said Yolanda. "If I can't perform, neither can you two."

"Look," argued Madelene, "No one has to do anything daring, no backflips or whips."

Effy was about to say she'd done plenty of backflips off the barn roof, only they weren't really back *flips*. She'd fallen backward onto haystacks, and she'd just done this a couple of times, *and* they were by accident.

"Mama, Jacque and I don't want to sit out the performances because of your pulled shoulder." Madelene jumped off the swing. "Phineas will give us other jobs. We're the Great Yolandas, top performers. Would you have us cleaning cages and stables? This girl could stand on the aerial platform and push us back and forth or be a catcher."

But I need to do more than that to impress Phineas, thought Effy. Swinging between platforms looked easy enough on the posters. *All I'd have to do is hold on tight.* The petals of an idea began unfurling in Effy's mind.

Phineas had said, *"You are no circus performer, and I am no father."* If she became an aerialist ... was it possible that he could become a true poppa?

"If I perform, your children don't have to give up their act. This will be good for the circus," Effy said in her most convincing voice.

Yolanda said nothing. Effy shuffled uncomfortably from foot to foot, staring at Madelene's calculating smiles. She wasn't sure if she wanted Yolanda to agree or not.

"You know Jacque and I will be fine, Mama," said Madelene.

"We do need the higher pay," said Yolanda. "And the ringmaster did send her here to us."

Effy saw no point in saying that she'd sent herself.

"We don't need her." Jacque jabbed a finger in Effy's direction.

"Ah, but you do, even if she only passes the swings to you both," said Yolanda. "All of you, change out of your street clothes and start rehearsing."

As Yolanda left, Jacque turned to his sister and smirked. "Well, you heard her; she's very good at falling off the roof. I'm sure we can help her with that."

It was clear to Effy that Jacque would like nothing better than dropping her on her head. She said, "Don't forget, I *am* the ringmaster's daughter." She grinned wickedly as Jacque pressed his lips into a thin white line and stomped away. At least now he had a reason to dislike her.

Madelene frowned. "Drat, I had my weekly bath already. Now I have to get all sweaty again."

"Why don't you take another bath after rehearsal?" Effy ventured.

"Two buckets a week, that's all any of us get. Water is always in short supply in a circus." Madelene smiled. "And you've already used up your buckets."

Circus life was most disagreeable, indeed. It only got worse when Effy followed Madelene into her family's caravan, where she opened a trunk, unfolded lavender-scented tissue paper, and pulled out skimpy tights.

"I ... I can't wear that." Effy's face felt as if it was on fire. She stared at the leotard.

"Trust me, you need to be able to stretch and move." Madelene tossed the outfit to Effy.

Effy willed herself to put it on, but she just couldn't. "People would see my limbs and my ... my ..."

"Fine, shrinking Violet." Madelene shrugged. She dug deeper into the trunk, under more layers of tissue.

"If you're so shy, this might suit you. Only we're supposed to save these outfits for performances, so don't tear this or get it dirty."

Madelene handed Effy a satin camisole with matching lace-trimmed short pants. At least the pantaloons would reach down to mid-thigh. And she could still wear the costume over her leotard so she wouldn't feel quite so ... undressed. No one would see naked skin.

Not to mention, the outfit was a shimmery white with silver spangles. She rather liked it. But once she'd put it on, she could almost hear Miss Letitia Nettles say, "You look worse than a dancer in the Moulin Rouge."

Aunt Ada wouldn't have objected to the idea of wearing pantaloons on the outside, or at least, not in principle. She'd always said women's long tight skirts were ridiculous for walking.

But as for the short length of *these* bloomers ...

... Effy could only imagine poor Aunt Ada spinning in her grave.

CHAPTER TEN

THE LANGUAGE OF FLOWERS

Effy and Madelene spent the entire afternoon swinging back and forth on the low-hanging trapeze. Jacque never returned for the rehearsal, and Effy felt all the better for it. She began her lessons by balancing on the narrow fly bar of the trapeze as she swung back and forth. That was no more difficult than when she'd walked across the top fence rung of the pigpen on the farm, or when she'd scaled the picket fence back home when Aunt Ada wasn't watching.

Only ... fences and pigpen rungs were stationary. Swinging made all the difference. Madelene told her to hang upside down by her knees as Madelene pushed the swing from behind. All the blood drained to Effy's head, but Madelene kept her swinging. Still, Effy refused to quit, even when she'd become dizzy, and the backs of her knees ached. Then sweat on the backs of her knees caused her legs to slip.

"Careful," said Madelene. "If you fall, you'll get your costume dirty. Now reach out and grab the other swing."

So she could slide off and hit the ground? Madelene wouldn't care if Effy cracked her skull, except for the blood that might stain her outfit, of course. The truth of it: Effy was no aerialist. She couldn't imagine swinging upside down when the trapeze was positioned *twenty feet* in the air.

That is, until Madelene said, "You better just push us back and forth. You're not showing any talent. Besides, aerialists require courage."

Effy summoned all her grit and determination. "Start the other swing."

When the other trapeze crossed within her reach, Effy didn't hesitate. She reached out and grabbed the bar. Then she promptly slid off the swing, one hand hanging on, her other arm dangling uselessly beside her as her slippered feet hung above the sawdust.

"Try it again."

It appeared Madelene was determined not to stop until Effy broke her neck. But Effy did try it, again and again, and again, until she could time the swing of the bar, grasp it with both hands, and transfer from one swing to another.

The sun began sinking below the golden tree boughs. When the rattling of banging pans swept across the circus grounds, Madelene wiped sweat from her brow as if she'd been the one working non-stop on the trapeze. "That's the call for supper. Come on, I'm starved."

At the cook wagon, the long benches were set up under a wide tent. Effy noticed that the trestle bench where the boss-handler sat was the only one decorated with a mason jar used as a vase. It held a single red carnation. Miss Mabel stood over Mr. Jefferson, clearly waiting to see if he noticed his flower. It appeared to Effy that he only noticed his plate of steaming food.

"A red carnation means my heart aches for you," Effy pointed at the vase. Madelene shrugged her shoulders and lined up in front of the cook.

"Ah, you understand the language of flowers," said the tiny woman standing behind Effy. She was the one Miss Mabel had called Miss Dot.

"Do you suppose Miss Mabel is dropping a hint to the boss-handler with that flower?" Effy bent over and whispered into Miss Dot's ear. "I'm not sure Mr. Jefferson understands."

Miss Dot reached up and patted Effy's hand. "I think you're right; he is clueless about carnations. And yet," she paused, "I think he is sweet on Mabel as well. I can't be sure. Too bad, as nothing would make Mabel happier."

Miss Dot sighed, and then looked into Effy's eyes. "Lots of folks can't express their true feelings, and it gets them into all sorts of misunderstandings."

Effy couldn't help but wonder if Miss Dot meant something more than the boss-handler and Miss Mabel's romantic difficulties. Miss Dot was the one who'd proclaimed Effy had a bone to pick with Phineas. Actually, Effy calculated, she had a whole boneyard to pick with him.

"Beans again?" A circus hand slammed his tin plate back on the table. The plate rattled and spun onto the ground.

"Don't have to eat it if you don't like it," grumbled Mr. Jefferson.

"We've been havin' beans for lunch and supper every night," said another man. A few others joined in with their complaints.

"When's the last time we've been fed a bit of meat?"

"Or saw a big bowl of potatoes?"

"Or ate anything besides molasses, beans, and cornbread?"

More circus folk murmured their agreement.

"If you don't appreciate Cook's food, or for that matter, Mabel's fine dinners, then you best keep it to yourself," the boss-handler warned them.

Effy noticed the happy blush on Miss Mabel's cheeks from Mr. Jefferson's praise. She turned to see if Miss Dot had noticed, but she had already joined another table and was fully into another conversation.

"Phineas had best turn more profit soon," Madam Vadoma said to Miss Mabel. "Circus folk don't appreciate this skimping on their food." More people came and sat on benches. Diners reached for forks as they swatted away ornery wasps and slow-moving blue bottle flies.

"I don't mind beans," Effy told Madelene as she took her second helping that day. She sat on a bench, wishing there was more cornbread left to scrape the plate clean. "These are truly tasty."

"Jacque also loves beans," said Madelene. "But beans give him dreadful wind, and when we're on the trapeze, and he's dangling from his knees"—she shook her head—"he lets out a colossal toot. Your eyes water like you're peeling onions. Trust me," Madelene added. "When he toots and you're on the trapeze, you won't be able to hold on."

That bit of information did not help when Effy and Madelene returned from supper, only to find Jacque waiting for them. As if he'd overheard Madelene, Jacque said, "Myself, I feel I've eaten too much. Don't you find it hard to turn away from a delicious plate of beans and molasses?"

Jacque promptly sat on the trapeze, and swung upside down with his rear end swinging back and forth, too close for Effy's comfort. "What are you waiting for," he said. "Lean forward and give me a push."

As he broke a loud toot, Effy scrambled backward and plugged her nose.

"Jacque, you're not funny." Madelene also plugged her nose.

Jacque slid from the swing and broke into howls of laughter. "You know what would be *much* funnier—if we were swinging twenty feet in the air."

Effy gulped. She needed to convince Phineas to send her away to school ... and soon.

Lanterns lit the caravans as most circus folk deserted the midway for the comfort of their beds. Some workers bunked under wagons. Jacque, Madelene, and their mother piled into a red caravan and left Effy standing by the trapeze rigs, wondering where she'd sleep. Shrugging, she set out for Phineas's wagon.

When she passed the menagerie, she heard the

restless pacing of Balally in her pen. Effy approached the hay-strewn ground, but stopped in her tracks and took several steps backward. In the murky dark, she spotted the shadowy outline of a great beast standing under the lantern pole. The elephant's foot was chained to a stout post. The chain strained as she paced back and forth. The water-boy made soothing noises until the elephant settled. He began rubbing the elephant's leg, which was thick as a tree stump.

"There, there, girl, I know you miss your elephant friends. It has been lonely for you since we joined this circus. Tell you what," he whispered to the elephant, as if he was confiding in a person. "I'll give you extra hay for your breakfast."

The elephant chirped softly. Effy watched in astonishment as the elephant reached into the boy's pocket with the tip of her trunk and plucked out an apple. The boy chuckled.

"Yes, that is your special treat, but I was saving it until after our goodnight song." The elephant had a different opinion. She tipped her trunk into her mouth and snapped the apple in a single crunch.

Never before had Effy seen such an enormous creature. Yet how gently Balally raised her trunk and stroked the boy's head, making clicking sounds, like a mother sending her child off to bed. Then she used the tip of her trunk like fingers and plucked a single strand of straw from the boy's hair.

The boy rubbed Balally's trunk as he sang her a soft lullaby in a language that sounded both beautiful and strange. The elephant's enormous ears twitched, and she swung her trunk in Effy's direction. Feeling like an eavesdropper, Effy backed away.

A roar made her jump. She spun around. A woman stopped a circus worker and said, "Could you move our cage away from the midway? My tiger's agitated being so close to the elephant pen."

"Not now," said the worker. "Everyone else is already bunked down for the night. Cover up its cage, and we'll get onto it in the morning, right after the parade."

"Be sure you do," said the woman. "I don't fancy working with a nervous tiger in my act."

Effy gaped in wonder. "A woman tiger tamer," she whispered, as if to make herself believe it. How could Aunt Ada disapprove of a circus where women did things most men wouldn't dare?

Effy made her way between the last rows of caravans before she stood outside the ringmaster's wagon. Not ringmaster, she told herself, *father*. She climbed two steps and banged on the door.

"Go away, I'm busy," shouted Phineas.

She knocked again.

"I said, go away."

"Excuse me, sir," Effy gulped, "but we need to talk."

The door flew open and Phineas stepped out. He no longer wore his red coat, but stood in white shirttails that hung past his knees. Dark circles smudged his eyes, and he rubbed his ink-stained fingers into his hair. "What are you doing here? I thought I sent you back on the train."

"First, there's only one train, and it's pulling out of the station as we speak," Effy felt compelled to explain. "Besides, remember, Madam Vadoma bid you let me stay."

Effy hoped Phineas didn't check in again with Madam Vadoma. She was pretty sure the mystic would tell him to send her packing.

"I thought you didn't like circuses. Why are you dressed up?" Phineas pointed to Effy's trapeze costume.

Effy felt her cheeks heat up as she tugged her baggy bottoms closer to her knees.

"Careful you don't tear that leotard," warned Phineas. "I suppose you wanted a costume for the circus parade." Then he said in a weary voice, "Everyone loves a parade."

"I don't, not particularly, unless of course it's a suffragist march. I was in one the day dear Aunt Ada ..."

"There you are," said Mr. Jefferson. "Mabel has me looking all over for you. I'm supposed to give you this." He climbed a step and handed Effy her embroidered bag. "Come and get settled for the night."

"I assumed I'd be staying with my ..." Effy heard the click of a latch and turned her head. Phineas had already gone back inside.

The boss-handler didn't meet her eyes. He cleared his throat and said softly, "He's a busy man. We won't see much of him before the first show."

"Everyone keeps telling me he's busy," Effy said. "He keeps telling me that. But I haven't seen him do anything." That didn't sound right. "I mean ..."

"Thinking is what your pa does most around here," said Mr. Jefferson. "Balancing books and acts, and running numbers, and finding a way to keep us going one more season—and to do that, he doesn't wish to be disturbed."

"We seem to have gotten off on the wrong foot." Effy sighed. "Perhaps I could stay with Miss Mabel?"

Jefferson chuckled as he shook his head. "Madam Vadoma is her bunk mate, and you've definitely got off on the wrong foot with her. For not being raised by him, you and Phineas are a lot alike."

She felt as alike to Phineas as a cat to a watermelon. As the boss-handler bid her follow, she asked him to wait a moment. Effy walked to the edge of the field next to the caravan and picked a handful of carnations someone had planted there.

Strewing the flowers across the ringmaster's steps, Effy then hurried after Mr. Jefferson. Looking over her shoulder, she wondered if Phineas understood the language of flowers.

Yellow carnations: *You have disappointed me.*

CHAPTER ELEVEN

ALMOST EVERYONE LOVES A PARADE

Effy and Mr. Jefferson approached a caravan painted almost as exotically as Phineas's quarters. Mysteries of the Orient were stencilled in bold black letters across the side. Dancing above the letters like sugar plum dreams, or perhaps nightmares, was a steaming cauldron with ghostly, devilish spirits. What would Aunt Ada have thought? Effy shook her head. The truth of it: Effy was in such a different world now, she was on her own. Aunt Ada could no longer guide her.

Mr. Jefferson climbed two wooden steps and pushed open the caravan's door. Inside, the wood floor gleamed shiny and clean, but Effy had to shove her way through diabolical-looking curios, including small sarcophagi and mummified rabbits. Effy imagined if she entered a crypt, it would have the same dry, old smell. A wood cot was built into the back of the caravan.

"I tidied this prop wagon for you," said Jefferson.

Tidied? Effy lifted a wooden puzzle box off the bed and placed it next to what she hoped wasn't a real monkey sitting on a shelf.

Effy jumped back. "Is that a coiled serpent in the corner?"

Mr. Jefferson followed her gaze but didn't appear alarmed. "It's stuffed," he said.

Effy tried not to shudder as she used her foot to push the leathery diamond-back snake further into the shadows.

"Careful there, it's considered bad luck to touch other people's circus props." Mr. Jefferson directed her to the cot. "Try not to disturb things."

Herbs hung from the ceiling. Dried flowers filled dusty mason jars—ingredients fit for a hag's cauldron. This caravan was nothing like her own cozy room at Aunt Ada's, but it was ... interesting. Also on the shelf was a single slim book. Effy reached over. "I'm supposing this book isn't a prop." She smiled and said with amusement, "Unless it's a grimoire of magic spells."

Mr. Jefferson chuckled and placed her bag on the floor. He reached over and lit a kerosene lantern. The flickering yellow light cast dancing shadows of monkeys and mummies and snakes.

Effy gazed at the shadows and decided if she didn't

want nightmares, she should keep her eyes on the book. Although Samuel Taylor Coleridge's *Book of Poems* did not entice Effy at first. This was the only book? She frowned.

Truth be told, Effy was to poetry as Aunt Ada had been to whale books. Generally speaking, Effy steered clear. A poem was usually mushy romance or glorified battles. Or a poem was really good, but over, just as it had whetted her appetite. Effy flipped open the cover, wondering if she should reread one of her own books. Then she read the first page and sank onto her bunk.

Effy became so engrossed in the ghostly tale of a cursed sailor, she never noticed Mr. Jefferson leave. "The Rime of the Ancient Mariner" definitely wasn't bedtime reading. After ten pages, she buried herself into her bunk, twisted the knob on the kerosene lamp, and the flame winked out.

The caravan was less spooky without the dancing shadows.

"Curses aren't real, curses aren't real," she whispered to herself in the pitch dark. "And superstitions are nonsense." Those thoughts didn't help her drift into a sweet and peaceful sleep.

Instead, Effy dreamed she was on a ship of living corpses, just like in the poem. The cursed albatross that hung around her neck had a face resembling Phineas's. By the time sunlight spilled through the cracks of the window shutter, Effy's bedcovers were twisted in knots. Her bangs stuck to her sweaty forehead. For one second, she thought she was still in the middle of her nightmare, and this was the hold of a cursed ship.

Then the door to the caravan banged and a voice said, "Hurry, everyone is already lining up for the circus parade."

Miss Mabel stuck her head through the door. "I see you're not an early riser. You'd best get dressed in your costume. Madelene says you're riding with the trapeze acrobats."

Miss Mabel frowned. "Watch your back with those two hooligans." Then she left.

Effy shook off the dreams that clung to her like sticky cobwebs. Yawning, she changed into the dratted trapeze costume with its leotard and spangled bloomers. A pair of wooden clogs sat outside her door, and she put them on to keep her acrobatic slippers clean. In the warm morning air, she crossed the circus grounds to the cook tent. Only Miss Mabel lingered.

"Sorry, dearie, you missed breakfast, but I managed to keep this for you." Miss Mabel was decked out in bright-coloured clothing and had oiled her beard until it gleamed in the morning light. She handed Effy an apple, paused, then reached into her apron and produced an orange. "This is from my private treasure—as valuable as gold in these parts."

Effy thanked her and tucked the fruit in the front pockets of her fancy spangled pantaloons. Then she hurried off to join the wagon train. The front of the line-up was already moving. As she passed a circus wagon near the back, Madelene waved her over.

"Get up here," she said with a sly smile. "You're riding with us."

After Effy climbed aboard the wagon, it occurred to her that while no one in the circus gave her costume a second glance, the town's folk would be a different story. Her heart began sinking as she thought about parading around town in her skimpy outfit. The horse-drawn wagon lurched forward and out onto the path.

Effy gripped the sides of the wagon. She had never stood on a moving wagon before. It was harder than it looked. The parade line snaked and twisted ahead as men in red coats marched, carrying trombones, trumpets, and a tuba. They wore large hats with plumed feathers, and the man at the rear beat a giant drum. Behind him marched acrobats tumbling cartwheels, and a strong man hoisting barbells. Then followed a blue and gold painted wagon pulled by a white horse. Standing on top of the horse with her arms outstretched was a rider in a netted skirt and purple tights. More circus performers rode inside the wagons or hung off them.

Effy spotted two people in the audience who made her heart sink to her clogs. Sofia and Mrs. Winterbottom stood behind a white picket fence that lined an elegant home. They waved lace hankies to keep the dust from their fancy frocks. While they gazed at white horses and acrobats, Effy ducked and dropped to the floor as the wagon lumbered past.

She heard Madelene say to her brother, "She thinks circus folk are not proper."

"No," Effy explained. "It's just that ... I'm not used to parading around in my underthings."

"I see." Madelene hung her head. "You're just like those awful people in the other town. You think someone like me doesn't even dress decently."

"No ..." Effy struggled to explain. "It's just that I met that girl and her mother on the train, and I don't want them to know ... I don't want them to think ..."

"... That you belong to the circus," snapped Madelene, "because circus folk aren't respectable."

The wagon rolled and lurched, and after they passed the next twist of the path, Jacque hauled Effy to her feet. He leaned in and whispered into her ear.

"So, you think *my* sister isn't respectable?"

Effy shook her head. "That's not it. The Winterbottoms think I'm off to an academy. Circus life is only temporary, a necessary step so Phineas will help me get back to my proper life."

After she'd said it, Effy realized that didn't sound quite right, either. The other two stared straight ahead as they all rode in grim silence.

Two wagons ahead, she spotted the elephant boy riding astride Balally. His uncle led the great beast. When the parade steered onto the main street, Effy gaped at all the people who had lined up to watch. It looked like the whole town had emptied its homes and businesses onto the main street.

She looked down once more at her pantaloons and leotard and felt her face heat up. She didn't crouch but edged further back in the wagon. Jacque looked at her scornfully and laughed.

The circus calliope broke into a steam-powered tune. Effy held tight as the wagon moved along the dirt road. A tiger roared, and when she turned and glanced at the cage rolling behind her, she felt a firm shove against her back. The next thing Effy knew, she was flying through the air.

Then everything went dark.

"I've got another one!" shouted a man. Effy opened her eyes and stared at a pair of dusty boots. The man leaned over her. His rumpled hat matched his wrinkled brown suit. "Smelling salts over here for the little lady who fainted," he shouted.

Effy's body ached from her toes to the tips of her hair. She gasped for air like a goldfish that had jumped its bowl. Then she groaned, "I didn't faint. I fell."

Had she? Or had someone pushed her off the circus wagon. She angled her head. A giant pile of elephant dung lay steaming on the dirt path a few feet away. This could have been a lot worse.

Effy lay on her back as another black cloud flooded her vision, but this time it was a murder of crows thick as a rain cloud. They flew overhead, chasing after an even bigger flock of sparrows. Conversations began ringing in her ears, and she could hear the calliope and the brass band in the distance. Her wagon was far ahead, and she'd been left behind in the dust.

"Fool parade," muttered the man in the brown suit.

"All sorts of people are fainting from shock at seeing an elephant." His voice trailed off as he looked down at Effy. His face reddened and he turned his head, "Quickly, please, bring some smelling salts over here!"

Effy lifted herself up on her elbows to see a woman in a long grey dress and a white starched apron rush toward her. The woman's hair was covered by a white frilly cap. She reached down, took the stopper out of a tiny cobalt bottle, and waved it under Effy's nose. Effy choked over the sudden sharp stench of ammonia.

"Ugh." Effy batted away the blue bottle.

The man in the brown suit hoisted Effy to her feet. She swayed. "Poor lamb, are you all right?" he asked. "Did the elephant scare you?"

"Gracious, child," said the woman. "I don't think you are here to watch the parade, not dressed in those immodest clothes." Her lips thinned in disapproval. "You better hurry back to your circus troupe where your, ah, wonton attire is deemed more appropriate."

The man in the brown suit pointedly looked away, and moved a few feet toward another figure on the ground.

"You thought hiring a nurse for the parade was a waste of money," the woman called after him, "but clearly all this excitement shows I'm needed here. Why, I myself almost swooned at the sight of that gigantic beast." She shook her head and hurried toward another bystander who had crumpled to the ground.

"Well, shucks, I certainly couldn't imagine the size of the elephant from a little-bitty page in a picture book," commented the man.

Effy dusted herself off with all the dignity she could muster. Several other people gaped at her in open curiosity. Her face burned as she watched the disappearing parade.

A long line-up of people had gathered along the grass-trampled trail at the end of the street. Near the end of the parade was Balally. On only slightly shaky legs, Effy followed the elephant.

When she finally caught up, the parade had emptied into the raised red-and-white striped circus tent. Only the elephant handler stood outside the entrance, leaning against the canvas tent, catching his breath.

Effy hurried inside the big top where the tidy parade line fell apart as the wagons pulled to a stop. Performers emptied into the arena. Effy kept moving across the sawdust, as flying splinters of wood poked through her stockings and inside her clogs. The back of her neck also felt prickly—the way it did when someone was staring at you. She turned around and saw two performers smirking at her.

... Madelene and Jacque ...

Effy's blood began to boil.

CHAPTER TWELVE

NOT JUST A KNOCKABOUT ACT

Performers hustled out of the big top. Effy and the trapeze hooligans paid little notice as they stood and glared at each other.

"Don't you know it's bad luck to look behind yourself in a circus parade?" Jacque scoffed.

"Why do I think I see bad luck right in front of me," said Effy. "Or more like I see a couple of *bad eggs*."

"How do you expect to balance on a trapeze when you can't even stand in a wagon?" Madelene shook her head.

"No one can stand in a wagon if someone pushes them," said Effy.

Madelene's eyes widened and she glanced at Jacque. The two of them exchanged a look that Effy didn't understand. Then without another word to her, the two raced off to rehearse once more before the first performance.

Effy wouldn't be left behind. She arrived at the trapeze rigging and grabbed a trapeze swing. She swung, switched bars, and grabbed the other trapeze swing. Madelene and Jacque pretended not to notice.

When Effy crossed onto the other platform, Madelene wouldn't move out of the way. Instead, she crossed her arms and said, "Go away. We don't need you."

"You do need me," Effy said evenly. "Or your mother won't let you perform."

Jacque laughed. "By the time Mama notices you aren't with us, she won't be able to stop our act. Then she'll see we're fine by ourselves."

"But you just watched me. I can swing from one bar to the other," Effy argued. "Besides, I've done dangerous things before. I dodged mounted police in a suffragist march."

"Oh, yes, I forgot how important you are." Madelene rolled her eyes.

"You never intended letting me perform, did you?" Effy accused.

Jacque grabbed a bar and swung off the platform. Madelene dipped her hand in a bucket and rubbed rosin onto her hands.

Effy refused to be ignored. She placed her hands on her hips. "I am a circus performer. Please get out of my way."

"You might be a rich girl and the ringmaster's daughter, but you are no aerialist," said Madelene.

Jacque swung lazily back and forth on his swing. He hung upside down on the bar and grabbed the rig Madelene pushed to him. He crossed back onto the low platform, which was now too crowded for Effy's liking.

"Go sit in the audience with your snooty friend and her mother," said Jacque. He made like he was about to give her a little shove. When she backed away, he laughed. "You'll be more comfortable sitting in the bleachers with the rubes, and not up on the platform with a couple of carnival ruffians. You won't have to wear a costume then. You'll be able to wear your fine and fancy dress."

"How can you thrill the audience with only the two of you?" Effy's mind raced. "I heard your mother. She said you weren't allowed to use any acrobatics without her."

Phineas had said Effy could be no performer and he could be no father. She had to perform. What could she say to convince these two that they needed her and not the other way around?

"For your act to be worthy of the Great Yolandas," said Effy, "you'll need to make the audience gasp in delight. How will you do that with a few simple swings on the fly bar?"

Madelene bit her lip. "This snobby girl has a point."

Jacque glared at them both. "She can barely hang onto the rigs. Her hands aren't even calloused."

"I'm standing right here." Effy was about to say her hands used to be plenty calloused on the farm. But Jacque's gripe about her good clothes had sent her thoughts spinning. He'd given her the kernel of a grand scheme. Why, with this spectacular plan, she wouldn't even have to wear an embarrassing leotard.

"What if ..." Effy rubbed her hands together. One of her fingers did so have a callous. "... What if, in the middle of your act, you pluck an unsuspecting girl—me," she said, in case this wasn't clear—"from the audience. You take me up onto the platform. Pretend you whisper in my ear what to do. Imagine how the audience will shout in trepidation. And when I stand on the bar and begin swinging, everyone will fall out of their seats in terror."

Jacque cocked his head. He was listening. Madelene gave the slightest of nods. Effy had best drive her point home. "This way, the audience gets thrills *and* chills, and when we take a bow, the audience will realize it's all part of the act."

Jacque's eyes sparked with interest. "If our act has a performance trick, then it won't just be a knockabout act."

Madelene nodded. "It will be worthy of the Great Yolandas."

Jacque huddled with Madelene and said something in her ear. She shook her head, then he whispered fiercely. She sighed. He looked up at Effy and smiled, but it wasn't a *We're all in this together* smile. Instead, it was as if he was in on the most interesting joke in the world.

Effy swallowed twice. It felt like a lump of sawdust got caught halfway down her throat. A twinge of doubt rose in her mind, but she stamped it down.

"Fine." Madelene turned to Effy. "But when you join us, just sit on the fly bar and swing from one side to the other. I will push you, and Jacque will catch you on the other side."

Effy nodded in agreement.

"Wear your most hoity-toity outfit and your finest boots, but not your gloves," said Jacque. "You don't want to slip on the ropes. The net is a long way down." He sauntered off.

Effy did a double take. Was that a threat? Madelene noticed Effy's hesitation and grabbed her hand. "Don't worry," she said. "I won't let him push you or let you fall. You will come to *no* harm."

Effy supposed that was reassuring.

Although it would have been more reassuring if Madelene hadn't needed to say anything at all.

CHAPTER THIRTEEN

HER MORTIFICATION

The sun was setting and there was no time to lose. People had already lined up to purchase tickets under the banner that said "The Great Rimaldi Circus." After a measly supper of a slice of bread with a dribble of molasses, Effy prepared for her act. Inside her wagon, she kicked off her clogs, or what the acrobats called slop shoes. With great happiness, she tore off the dratted leotard and changed into her green silk dress, frilled bloomers, and stockings. Effy laced up her boots.

A thorough bag search didn't produce a hairbrush. Perhaps in her haste to bring her favourite books, Effy had forgotten to pack one. She plucked sawdust chips from her hair. Once she was presentable, Effy took the back way around the tent and slipped into the striped big top. She took a seat in the audience. No one noticed her, not even Phineas, as the other performers got in position for the show to begin.

The murky light inside the canvas tent cast dream-like shadows. As if part of the dream, Effy imagined sailing through the air on the flying trapeze. Everyone would be amazed. This was the perfect plan, and it would be a most satisfying moment to see the surprise on the ringmaster's face.

If only her stomach would agree.

The single slice of bread had turned into a heavy lump. She had Miss Mabel's apple and precious orange tucked in her dress pockets for later, and now she was glad she hadn't eaten them.

Handlers pulled back the entrance flap and a cool breeze filtered through the tent. Townsfolk streamed into the big top and took their seats on the benches. Effy's heart beat quickly as she kept her gaze fastened on the circus ring. The brass band blared, and when a marching tune swelled, Phineas strode into the arena.

Phineas commanded the attention of the audience with the crack of his whip. Taking off his top hat, the ringmaster bowed to the crowd, then placed the hat back on his head. The crowd cheered. Effy looked at the people sitting beside her. She saw marvel on their faces. Could Aunt Ada have been mistaken? Was there more to Phineas than flimflam and nonsense?

With another snap of the ringmaster's whip, horses and acrobats circled the ring. Effy gasped as the acrobats jumped from one white horse to another. One woman did a handstand on a galloping horse, showing more derring-do than any cowboy in any Wild West show back on the farm.

Clowns with floppy shoes, white greasepaint, and red rubber noses cavorted with the audience between acts. They bumbled and bounced off each other, and some poked fun at the townsfolk. One clown grabbed a child's bag of popcorn, but handed it back when the girl hollered.

With another crack of the whip, Phineas bellowed for the audience to watch the tiger tamer in the cage with her tiger. Effy barely took a breath as she watched the tiger jump through rings. The tiger roared, reminding everyone it was a wild beast that could tear off the trainer's arm with a single bite.

The big top had such a mesmerizing effect on Effy that she looked up in surprise when Jacque tugged her arm. It took her a moment to remember what he wanted. He pulled her to her feet.

A hush fell over the audience as Effy crossed the sawdust floor. She decided in a snap that she wouldn't avoid the truth of it. Her legs were more than a little wobbly. She told herself how everyone was going to be surprised when she got up onto that platform and swung from the trapeze, especially Phineas.

Jacque flew up the rope ladder while Effy took one rung at a time. People had already started gasping, especially when the rope wobbled. She smiled to herself and warmed to the performance. Effy began making the most of a few bumbles and stumbles. Halfway up, she twisted the ladder around and was rewarded with shouts of fear.

She'd stumbled too well, and the ringmaster strode toward her. Effy then flew up the rest of the rungs as fast as a squirrel scrambling up a tree.

Madelene and Jacque were already on the other platform. Effy looked down, way down, to the net below, and swallowed as her heart banged against her ribs.

Jacque and Madelene swung and changed bars on the trapeze. At one point, Jacque hung upside down and caught Madelene. If the audience applauded, Effy didn't hear.

It also didn't matter that handlers were shouting at each other as they stared up at the ropes. It didn't matter that Phineas stood below and demanded she come straight back down. It didn't matter that the horses neighed restlessly as the acrobats circled the outer ring and watched her, or that the caged tiger roared.

Effy hardly heard any of it. Sounds faded as blood banged against Effy's eardrums.

"Hurry," urged Madelene, handing her the fly bar. "You can't hesitate. You know that by now. This is a simple swing. And for pity's sake, don't stand. Make sure you stay seated."

Effy's confidence had evaporated like spilled lemonade on a hot day. She even felt the stickiness of her sweat. So what if she'd climbed plenty of ladders on the farm, or swung from tree branches? She'd trusted only herself then, and not these two, who'd let her fall like Humpty Dumpty.

She was sure Jacque had pushed her from the circus wagon so she would land in a giant pile of elephant manure—which would have been worse than where she landed, despite her bumps and bruises.

Effy decided in a snap that to be safe, she'd swing to the other platform and jump off *before* Jacque caught her. Effy grabbed a handful of rosin and rubbed it onto her palms. She stepped on the trapeze.

"I said sit on the bar," urged Madelene.

Effy slid down and sat. Her fists turned white as she gripped the rope. Madelene pushed hard and Effy swung from the platform. The audience gasped in delight.

Effy pumped her legs and swung toward the other platform. But she brought her knees sharply back just as Jacque reached out. She wouldn't deny the truth of it, his annoyed grimace made her smirk.

On her second swing, Effy gripped the ropes and pulled herself to stand on the swing. She was rewarded by more gasps, even screams and shouts—although the shouts were possibly from Phineas. Couldn't the ringmaster see she was a fine aerialist?

"Boots are too stiff for a fly bar," Madelene hissed when Effy swung back.

Too late, Effy's boot slipped, and her leg and arm dangled from the swing as she clung to the rope with her other hand.

People screamed. Perhaps she was one of them.

Effy gripped with all her might and pulled herself upright on the bar. Then she slid back down to a sitting position. As she struggled to centre herself, she didn't have time to pull back her knees.

Jacque leaned forward and grabbed Effy by her boots. He tugged Effy straight off the swing and hung her upside down.

Effy's skirts and petticoats covered her head. The

audience burst into laughter. Her face burned with mortification. She could feel her bloomers slide up past her knees and edge toward total disaster—her bare thighs.

The audience chortled and bellowed. A thump landed above Effy. Another pair of hands grabbed her behind the knees and pulled her up to the platform. Her face blazed, but it wasn't from all the blood rushing to her head.

Jacque smirked. "Don't you know it's bad luck to wear green in a circus act?"

Effy fumed, but she had no choice. She had to climb down the ladder and take her place centre ring with the two hooligans. The audience still roared with laughter. When the three of them bowed, Effy couldn't bring herself to look up at the people in the stands. What if Sophia or Mrs. Winterbottom had attended? Nor could she cast her gaze at Phineas, who was muttering words like "disaster" and "dangerous," and other words of which Aunt Ada would strongly disapprove.

Instead, she ran from the ring and looked nowhere but at the sawdust beneath her feet.

CHAPTER FOURTEEN

THE RINGMASTER'S WRATH

Effy stumbled as she ducked through the canvas flap at the back exit—what the performers called clown alley. The sky spun like a top before she regained her footing. She steadied herself against a huge pillar.

"Watch out!" shouted Miss Dot.

Effy twisted around. It wasn't a pillar. It was the elephant's limb—which was ... very ... big. Circus folk gasped. Someone laughed—she suspected Madelene.

Effy gulped and lurched away. She had to admit the truth of it. While she wasn't unschooled in the size of elephants, standing this close made her realize in a whole other way just how gigantic this elephant was.

Balally had been painted for the parade and the show. Her chalky white trunk snaked toward Effy and arched over her head. The trunk hovered there a second, then crept down Effy until the tip reached her front pocket.

"Don't move!"

"The elephant's attacking the ringmaster's daughter."

"The elephant's getting ready to attack us all!"

Effy froze. People backed away. A man hollered, "Stop shouting or you'll spook the elephant and make her stampede!"

Someone else said, "Cuthbert, git over here. Where's your uncle?

Cuthbert dropped his water buckets near the back exit. He raced toward Effy and the elephant.

Balally searched Effy's pocket and plucked out her orange. In one flex of her trunk, Balally dropped the orange into her mouth. The second time the elephant's trunk arced, Effy quickly pulled the apple out of her other pocket and held it up. "Here," she gulped. "Please, help yourself."

"Balally loves your fruit more than I loved my mother's curried fish roti," Cuthbert joked. Then he quickly added, "Please stay calm."

"I'm perfectly calm," Effy lied.

The shouting man reached over to bat Cuthbert's ear, but Cuthbert stepped aside. "No sudden movements, please, sir."

The man backed away. Balally gently grazed her trunk over Cuthbert's hair and shoulder.

"It's a menace," said the man, once he stood at a safer distance. "We all could have been trampled."

A few other performers murmured in agreement.

"Where is the elephant handler?" Mr. Jefferson waded through the mob of performers who'd circled them. "The acrobats are riding again because he hasn't taken Balally out to the ring."

He spotted Cuthbert and said, "Do you know where your uncle is? He'd never leave his elephant alone like this."

Worry furrowed Cuthbert's brow. "I haven't seen him since the parade. I'll look for him."

"The show must go on," Mr. Jefferson said, firmly but gently.

Cuthbert sucked in his breath and gently urged his elephant toward the entrance. "I'll ride her."

Effy remembered that after the parade, she'd seen the elderly handler leaning against the canvas by the big top entrance. Now, exiting the big top, she spotted the crumpled figure sitting on the ground and hurried toward him. "Mr. Jefferson, Miss Mabel. Someone, please help!"

The old man struggled for breath. Mr. Jefferson came running, with Mabel and Madam Vadoma right behind him.

"I am fine," the elephant handler said, waving his hand to shoo them away. "I ... just had one of my spells."

"What sort of spells would that be, Amal?" asked Mr. Jefferson as he helped him up.

The old man wheezed. "I simply needed a rest. That is all."

"Elephants can't be left wandering about on their own, especially during a performance," Mr. Jefferson said, not unkindly. "If this happens again ..."

"No need to worry," said the elephant handler. "I am fine now. And listen how the audience claps for my nephew. All is well."

Miss Mabel sent a worker to fetch water for Mr. Amal. More performers gathered. When everyone looked at Effy, they either chuckled or whispered to each other.

"Say it to my face," Effy said through gritted teeth. Her cheeks burned, but it was best to get her humiliation over with and move on.

"You mean that the ringmaster finally met his match?" Miss Mabel smiled.

That wasn't what Effy had expected they'd been saying.

Mr. Jefferson snorted, then took his cap off and wiped his forehead with his bandana. "We shouldn't be laughing, though. Phineas is storming around and looks like he's swallowed a bucket of hot coals."

"Those trapeze terrors have crossed the line." Miss Mabel dropped her voice. "It was only a matter of time before they stirred the ringmaster's wrath."

"Poor Yolanda." Madam Vadoma sighed. "Vat vill happen to them now?"

You're the fortune teller, thought Effy.

The show had ended and townsfolk poured out of the tent. Effy took her leave and circled around the big top, away from the midway. She'd only been thinking of her great mortification. Angering the ringmaster had never occurred to her. It was all Jacque and Madelene's fault. Effy spotted them loitering backstage in clown alley, near the animal pens.

"Sneaks, wretches!" Effy shouted at them. "I hope the ringmaster dumps a vat of molasses over your heads, rolls you in chicken feathers, and runs you out of town. I should ..."

Effy pulled to a stop. She hadn't noticed Phineas and Yolanda standing there.

Madelene hung her head. Her long black ringlets fell past her waist. Jacque's face had taken on a greenish tinge. Phineas's complexion had darkened to magenta.

Yolanda wrung her hands together. "You've gone too far," she snapped at the trapeze terrors. "The ringmaster was the only one who would take us in. So, how do you repay him? You almost kill his daughter."

Phineas put his hand on her shoulder. "I'm sorry, Yolanda, but that was a calamity wrapped up in a disaster. This time I must ..."

"It was my idea," said Effy.

Everyone's head swooped in her direction.

"What?" said Phineas.

Effy swallowed. "The act was my grand scheme. Jacque and Madelene needed a trick so they wouldn't perform a boring knockabout act. So, I suggested they pull me from the audience. And we'd pretend I'd almost fall." *Except it wasn't all pretend.*

Phineas's bushy eyebrows drew together like a giant caterpillar glued to his forehead. He took a step toward her.

Effy struggled but found her voice. "And my plan worked ... ah, mostly."

"The audience loved it," said Madelene.

"They were howling with ..."

"Stop." Yolanda held out her hand, cutting off Jacque.

Phineas reached over and grasped Effy's chin. He lifted her face up to his until she couldn't look away from his icy stare. "You will never step inside that circus ring again. Am. I. Clear?"

Effy would have nodded but he'd locked hold of her chin. She said, "You are clear."

Phineas spun around and stormed away.

from his levitate. "You will never step inside that circus
ring again, Aunt Claudia."

Effy would have called out, made a physical hold of her
chin. She said, "You must gra—"

CHAPTER FIFTEEN

THE EYE OF THE TIGER

Effy intended to go straight to her wagon and stay out of
the ringmaster's way. That was the truth of it. But she'd
cut through the animal menagerie and couldn't resist
stopping by the elephant pen. Inside the small, fenced
area, Cuthbert led his elephant to a tethering post and
fastened her leg to a long chain.

"I found your uncle," Effy reassured him. "He said
he had one of his spells. Miss Mabel and Miss Vadoma
are tending him, though he says he's fine now."

Cuthbert nodded, but his face was pinched with
worry. With a start, Effy saw Balally sense his dismay
and stroke his hair with her trunk.

Effy had never given much thought to horses pulling
carts, or cats and dogs roaming the neighbourhood, or
the chickens she'd argued with every morning on the
farm. This elephant's tenderness surprised her.

"I think your elephant loves you with all her heart,"

said Effy, climbing up on the top rung of the fence.

"An elephant's heart is very big, so I am lucky." Cuthbert handed Balally a handful of straw. "I see you are fearless of my elephant. That you sense how gentle she is."

Effy had perched herself on a rung just short of where the elephant's trunk could reach. Or at least, that's what she thought. The elephant arced her trunk and laid it on Effy's chest. As her heart pounded, Balally lifted the tip of her trunk toward Effy's face, as if giving her a good sniff. Cuthbert had called Effy fearless, so she did her best not to flinch.

"Balally's taken to you," Cuthbert said.

"Um, how nice." Effy tried but failed not to sound flustered.

Cuthbert steered Balally away as he laughed. "She takes some getting used to."

When this boy laughed, it was with a kindness totally lacking in Jacque's cruel taunts.

"I ... I overheard you yesterday at Phineas's wagon. You were saying your elephant is in trouble." Effy frowned. "That you need the ringmaster to save her."

"Everyone is talking about you." Cuthbert smiled ruefully. "No one can believe ..."

"That I am the ringmaster's daughter." Effy shook her head.

"No, that he is a father," Cuthbert corrected.

"And yet, I am sorely in need of a father. Only ... Phineas is as much a father as I am a great circus performer." When Cuthbert was about to say something, Effy put up her hand.

"So, it's only logical that I figure out a dazzling circus act that will make me a circus performer extraordinaire. That way, I will win Phineas's affection, and can speak up for Balally."

Those were lofty promises, but there had to be a way to get Phineas to help her. Only it couldn't involve Effy stepping inside the circus ring. How would she become a performer now?

Effy returned to her wagon as the aches and disappointments of the day caught up to her. Once she'd changed into her nightgown, there was a soft knock on the door.

"Cook sent this for you," called Miss Mabel.

Effy opened the door as Miss Mabel handed her a bowl of turnip stew. Effy grabbed the spoon and dug in. All the livelong day, she'd had hardly a bite of food.

"Cook's fond of you," said Miss Mabel. "You're the

only one who doesn't complain about his cooking."

At least someone in the circus liked her, thought Effy. Effy almost heard Aunt Ada say in her no-nonsense voice, "You are not here to make friends, my dear Ephemia, you are here to convince your guardian to send you back to school."

"Tomorrow, I will do exactly that," Effy told herself as she crawled into bed. She only hesitated a moment before she turned off her lantern. Gaslights outside the wagon cast flickering shadows on the inside. She watched how the garish props of monkeys, snakes, and headless capes danced on the wall.

The next morning, Effy sat alone on the bench in the cook's tent. Jacque and Madelene stopped by for only a second.

"Don't think you're too good for me or my sister because you took the blame yesterday," said Jacque. "We don't need your charity. Besides, you only did it because you're the ringmaster's daughter, and he won't harm a hair on your head."

"You're very welcome," said Effy.

Madelene tugged her brother's arm. "Well, it's true," he said to his sister.

"I'm not so sure," said Madelene as they left.

Effy *hoped* the ringmaster was no longer angry. Anyway, all she needed was a new plan. She pocketed three apples and headed straight for the elephant's pen. As Effy rounded a circus wagon, she overheard the tiger tamer arguing with a circus handler.

"You told me yesterday you'd move my tiger's cage away from the elephant's pen," she said.

"I did get it moved," said the handler.

"I didn't mean a few more wagons away." The tiger tamer pointed across the field. "It needs to be clear on the other side of the camp or my beast will be agitated again tonight."

"I need to get a horse and more help for that," said the handler. "We're right busy at the moment."

"Do you wish to perform with my tiger tonight, when she's pacing and lashing her tail and growling?" the tamer said evenly.

"Right, then." The handler sighed. "I'm on it."

Effy climbed to the top rung of Balally's pen and held out the apples. The elephant scooped them up with her trunk. After she'd eaten the apples, Balally arched her trunk and patted Effy again on the head. Flustered, Effy lost her balance and slid off the rung into the pen. She landed on a bale of hay.

"You're sitting on Balally's breakfast," Cuthbert pointed out as he walked into the pen.

Effy scrambled over the fence and out of the pen.

"Balally won't take a bite of you—she's vegetarian." Cuthbert laughed. Effy laughed as well, but took several steps back when Balally raised her trunk and let out an ear-splitting trumpet.

"It's a blowout!" a man screamed.

Effy looked at Cuthbert.

"A disaster," Cuthbert said worriedly.

Effy turned and scanned the field and midway. "Oh," she gasped.

"Run," another man shouted. "The tiger cage tipped over and the tiger's escaped."

A roar cut across the circus grounds, a sound that would curdle anyone's blood. Worse, every other creature in the menagerie fell silent. Worse yet, one sound grew louder: growling.

"Kneel, Balally," Cuthbert commanded. He unlinked the elephant's chain. Then in an urgent voice, he said, "Quickly, ringmaster's daughter. Get inside the pen and climb into the howdah on top of my elephant. Hurry."

Cuthbert scrambled on top of Balally, but Effy couldn't join him; she couldn't even turn her back. Not if turning forced Effy to take her eyes off the approaching tiger.

Effy recalled reading somewhere that if you saw the yellow of a tiger's eyes—it was the last thing you ever saw.

If that was true, she had seconds to live.

CHAPTER SIXTEEN

IF I COULD BECOME A VETERINARIAN, I WOULDN'T BE FLYING A TRAPEZE

The great cat slammed to a halt in front of Effy. His tail whipped with irritation as his yellow eyes flicked back and forth. Other people screamed, but it was as if Effy's ears were plugged with cotton batting. Effy didn't breathe, didn't think, and didn't move; she held the tiger in her gaze.

A familiar feeling slid down her back—it was the elephant's trunk. This time, Effy didn't flinch when Balally coiled her trunk around her waist. It was easy for Effy not to gasp or call out as Balally lifted her in the air. Truth be told, whatever the elephant did would surely not hurt as much as a tiger's fangs and claws.

Effy soared over the elephant's shoulder until Cuthbert grabbed her arms and helped her scramble on top of the elephant and behind him, into the wide howdah.

"Clear the circus grounds," bellowed Phineas. The tiger roared as the ringmaster rushed forward. He halted, shouting, "Never mind. Stand still everyone, except the tamer and the handlers."

The tiger tamer cracked her whip and eyed the agitated beast. "He's spooked," said the woman, shaking her head. "He won't obey my commands."

The group of handlers, armed with shovels and rakes and pitchforks, backed away from her. One man muttered, "I'd need all my owed pay before I wrangle any tiger."

Only Mr. Jefferson stood alongside the tiger tamer, that is, he stood there until Miss Mabel grabbed both his shoulders and shoved him clear.

"Balally, forward," said Cuthbert. The elephant lurched.

"I know what you're doing," said Effy. "I read that elephants are nature's tiger wranglers."

"Exactly," said Cuthbert.

Balally took another step as Effy swayed on the platform strapped to her broad back. To keep from sliding off, she squeezed Cuthbert around the waist. The tiger stepped backward. Balally moved forward. Step by step, Balally forced the tiger toward the cage.

Effy could see there was one problem. The door of the cage had fallen shut when the wranglers had set it upright. There was no hope that any of the wranglers could squeeze between Balally and the escaped tiger and open the cage.

Effy looked to her left and saw that one of the handlers had a rifle and was aiming it at the tiger.

"No!" the tiger tamer cried out. "Please."

Effy's heart thudded. "Cuthbert, edge Balally closer to the cage."

Cuthbert obliged. Effy didn't think about what she would do next, because if she thought it out carefully, her courage would fail her. Instead, she slid off the elephant onto the top of the tiger cage.

"Tarnation, you foolish child," bellowed Phineas. "Don't you know the tiger can easily leap on top of that cage."

She hadn't realized that. But it was too late for second thoughts. Effy reached down and grabbed the cage door by the hinges. Hanging halfway down, Effy used both hands to swing the door open.

Balally lumbered forward, backing the hissing tiger nearer the opening. The tiger tamer started snapping her whip near the tiger's paws. This drove the snarling tiger the rest of the way inside the cage. Effy slammed the cage door shut.

A collective shout rang through the crowd. Everyone

clapped. Balally lowered herself to her knees, and Cuthbert climbed down. "Good work, Balally," Cuthbert kept repeating to his elephant.

Effy scrambled down from the cage, and the tiger tamer helped her onto the ground. Effy spotted Madelene and Jacque. Jacque whispered something into Madelene's ear as she kept her gaze on Effy. What were they plotting? Nothing good.

Someone spun Effy around. She was face-to-face with Phineas.

"If you ever"—Phineas said in a dead quiet voice that still sent shivers crawling across Effy's scalp—"put yourself in danger again: in the ring, on a fool trapeze, on the midway ... anywhere ...!"

"... I'll send you packing to a boarding house, myself." He stomped away.

Now what would she do? Phineas was angrier than ever.

Once the tiger was safely in his cage, most of the circus crowd scattered. Cuthbert stooped next to Balally's leg, looking deadly concerned. Effy hurried over.

"Balally's bleeding." Effy gasped. White chalk paint mixed with blood turned the elephant's limb into a pink, splotchy mess.

"The tiger got in a swipe with his claws," said Cuthbert.

"You need to wash all that paint off before Balally gets an infection."

Effy jumped at that voice and stepped back when Madelene brushed past her. The girl that Effy didn't trust a whit leaned over and gently patted the elephant's leg. She examined Balally's wounds.

"Careful," Effy warned her. "Balally's in pain. One stomp from an angry elephant and you'll be bug squash."

Madelene scoffed.

"They are friends," said Cuthbert. "Balally knows she's trying to help."

Effy glanced at the trapeze girl in surprise. Truly, she couldn't imagine Madelene having any friends, animal, vegetable, or mineral.

"There, girl, steady." Madelene grabbed a handful of field flowers and daubed the deep scratches. Balally looked down at her with soft brown eyes.

Madelene glanced at Effy, who quickly shut her gaping mouth. Madelene shrugged. "Animals are a lot nicer than people. They don't care if you're ..." She shook her head. "I'm just better with animals."

Madelene wiped around the wound. "This lavender should sooth Balally's wounds." She looked up at Cuthbert.

"We need to wash all the chalk off, or it will keep dribbling into the cuts."

"I could try and get more water." Cuthbert got to work, wiping away the chalk paint with his hand. He scowled. "But you know how the water handler is."

Madelene nodded. "Tell the handler this is an emergency. Your elephant was wounded in the line of duty."

"I can get you all the water you need," said Effy.

Madelene scoffed. "Of course, you can. You get special privileges, ringmaster's daughter. Jacque and I are in so much trouble from your little scheme. Mama is furious."

"What privilege? I am one step away from being sent back to my *vulturous* relatives." Effy gently patted Balally's injured leg. "I know of a fresh pond near the woods. Do you want more water or not?"

She pointed toward the falls she'd spotted from the tree where she'd slept her first night. "The pond's clean because it's filled by fast moving water spraying from a cliff."

"We need bandages and some herbs to make a salve," Madelene told Cuthbert, ignoring Effy.

"What sort of herbs?" What had Effy ever done to this angry girl, anyway?

"Yarrow grows here; do you even know what that looks like?" Madelene held Effy in her scornful gaze.

"Those tiny white flowers in the field," Effy said smoothly.

Madelene broke her stare and went back to tending Balally's leg. "And if you can, find some calendula. Also, ask Miss Mabel for honey to make the poultice."

Marigold was part of the calendula family, and Effy was sure she'd seen a jar of those dried flower heads in her caravan. She nodded. "You know a lot about healing. You could be a veterinarian."

Madelene stood, brushed spikey leaves off her hands and laughed bitterly. "If I could become a veterinarian, I wouldn't be flying a trapeze with my stinky brother."

"There are already two women doctors in Toronto." Effy brightened with her usual enthusiasm on woman and equality. "Dr. Emily Stowe and her daughter, and Clara Brett Martin just became Toronto's first woman lawyer. Soon there will be women in every profession. Just like men. We just have to speak up!"

Madelene looked at Effy with such hate, Effy took a step back.

"I don't need a lecture on women taking on men's work. Every woman in this circus knows she's equal to any man. Haven't you seen that for yourself?" Madelene shook her head. "But here you are spouting all your fancy facts."

"But I just meant ..." Effy stopped when she saw Madelene's eyes flash.

"Did it ever occur to you that those hoity-toity lady doctors and lawyers are from refined society and have special privileges?" said Madelene.

Actually, it hadn't. Effy shook her head.

"I didn't think so. Not all of us have rich family connections," said Madelene. "A fatherless girl from the circus won't ever get far."

"And it's not just girls. Not every boy can become an engineer." Cuthbert hugged his elephant's leg and sighed wistfully. "Some of us are from foreign lands. It's not easy. Not everyone wants us here."

"But the women's movement cares about others," said Effy. Madelene scoffed again, and Effy vaguely remembered a lecture from Miss Letitia on becoming moral guardians. That did sound like only *certain* people should be in charge.

Effy didn't know what else to say. She felt foolish. "I ... guess I never thought about much besides getting into a good school."

"Why would you?" said Madelene. "All my life, my family's been run out of towns because people like your family never think we are good enough. They call us riffraff. You don't like what happens with your fancy inheritance, so you hop on a train and run here to *our* home and act like we're all beneath you."

"That's not the whole truth of it," admitted Effy. "Before the circus, I just didn't think about being privileged." Effy looked at Balally. "Or how animals are important and have feelings."

Madelene stirred the sawdust with the toe of her boot. Then she looked long and hard at Effy. "At least you're honest. Maybe there's hope for you yet, uppity girl."

Maybe Effy was more uppity than she'd realized, but it was clear how Madelene and Cuthbert needed a say in their own lives, just like she did. And that Balally needed someone to speak up for her.

"We have to rehearse," shouted Jacque. "We get to perform. Mama's shoulder is better."

Jacque stood well away from the elephant. "Madelene, your timing is perfect. I've just finished another plate of beans."

"I have to go." Madelene sighed. "Do you think you can manage the poultice?"

"Clearly," said Effy, deep in thought.

Madelene shot her a strange look before she turned and hurried away.

CHAPTER SEVENTEEN
NO ONE IS COMING TO OUR RESCUE

As Cuthbert led his elephant to the water, Effy plucked a handful of the tiny white flowers she knew were yarrow. Then she raced back to the caravan where she found the jar of dried marigold. Her cotton petticoat would make excellent bandages. Her face still managed to heat up when she thought of Jacque dangling her upside down, for the entire circus to see her fine underthings.

Effy decided she'd give it no further thought. After all, this was a circus, where tiger tamer ladies wore britches and acrobats wore, well, she'd best never mind about that.

Effy went to find Miss Mabel at the cook's tent. "Miss Mabel, I'm in need of scissors and a pot of honey." She pressed her hand against the stitch in her side while she caught her breath.

Miss Mabel eyed the petticoat bundled under Effy's arm, but she fetched the scissors and gave them to Effy.

Miss Mabel scratched her chin under her long curly beard. "Cook wants me to ask why you need the honey. He only has one jar, making it rare as oranges in this circus."

"For Balally's wounds," said Effy.

"You're making a poultice, then." Miss Mabel took one more look at Effy's petticoat, shrugged, and headed inside the cook's tent. After a few heated words, she returned and handed over a sticky honey pot. "It's the least we can do after the elephant saved us all from the tiger."

Thanking her, Effy turned to race away, but Miss Mabel held her back one more second. The bearded lady stuffed two more apples into her pockets. "You also missed lunch."

Effy crunched half an apple with one bite as she ran toward her caravan. Then she collided with Mr. Jefferson.

He'd been carrying a ladder, but had set it down to remove his cap and wipe his forehead. He grabbed her arm and steadied them both. "That was a close call. Where are you off to like all creation?"

"Nowhere." Effy almost choked on her apple. She had no time for chit-chat.

"Were you coming from the cook's tent?"

Effy nodded.

"What did you want with Mabel?" Mr. Jefferson eyed

the jar of honey. "She's not one for doling out honey, even if you are the ringmaster's daughter."

Effy swallowed the rest of her apple. "The honey's for emergency uses only." Then she had a thought and stopped mid-stride. "I think you don't care about the honey. Are you asking because you're curious about Miss Mabel?"

Mr. Jefferson blushed.

"You're sweet on her." Effy clapped her hand over her mouth, realizing she'd said that aloud.

Mr. Jefferson cleared his throat. "She *is* a very fine-looking woman."

"Even though she has a beard?" Once again words flew out of Effy's mouth, and she wished she could take them back. Miss Mabel was kind, and it was not proper to comment on her difference. Effy had been raised better.

"I ... I'm sorry, ah, again." Her cheeks heated up.

Mr. Jefferson laughed. "Mabel has a beard until she retires to her wagon at nightfall. Then she takes it off. In the morning, she glues it back on."

"Oh." Effy hadn't guessed. A circus, it seemed, was like a magic show. Illusion was what caught people's attention and drew them in.

Mr. Jefferson picked up the ladder. "She's a fine, handsome woman, anyway. A beard wouldn't matter."

Effie held on for one more moment. "Why don't you tell her how you feel?"

"Oh, I ... couldn't." Mr. Jefferson's voice faded as if he had laryngitis. "I ... could never find the words."

Effy smiled. "There are carnations bordering the farmer's field, by Phineas's wagon. Go there and pick Miss Mabel a bouquet of red ones. If you hand her those, you won't need to say a single word."

Miss Mabel would understand. Red carnations—*my heart aches for you.* Effy rushed away. If a man didn't give a fig as to whether or not a woman had a beard, Effy decided he'd probably make a passable husband.

She followed the trail to a small clearing. The sharp smell of fast-moving water sprayed down the two jutting cliffs. When she stepped through a thin grove of flaming red maple trees, she spotted the elephant cavorting in the large pond. Balally trilled and chirped in unmistakable glee as she paddled. Once again it struck Effy how Balally had all the heart and joy of any person she'd met—perhaps even more so.

"Balally hasn't had a good bath in so long." Cuthbert looked as if someone had given him the best gift ever. "She ... deserves this." He choked on those last words.

The elephant lifted her trunk and playfully sprayed

water at them. Laughing, Effy thought this was the closest she'd get to washing up. If only she'd brought a stick of lye soap with her. Balally waded deeper and floated. Effy marvelled that an elephant's face could show such bliss, or at least, that's how it looked. Cuthbert, knee-deep in the pond, kept a close eye on his elephant.

Effy longed to dive in. She hadn't been swimming in a pond since her farm days, when no one cared what she did in those slivers of time between chores. Only she didn't dare wet her plain pinafore dress. She really ought to have packed more clothes. She surprised herself by thinking longingly of the short bloomers and top she'd worn in the parade. How those would be perfect for swimming.

Effy sat on the shore, imagining she floated in the pond's cool depths. She began tossing rocks into the water, watching how her single rock caused a series of circles spreading wider and wider. Aunt Ada had once told her that every leaflet they handed out, every march they attended spread the idea of women's rights wider and wider. Like her skimming rocks in a pond.

If only everyone could embrace those ideas. Not just privileged girls like Madelene supposed Effy was. Privileged? Why, she was only one step away from cooking and scrubbing clothes, and cleaning day and night in a boarding house.

After Balally reluctantly climbed on the shore, Effy patched the wounds on the elephant's limb. She applied crushed marigold and yarrow, slathered a barrier of honey, and wrapped Balally's leg in the long winding strips of her petticoat.

"You also have the skills of a healer," Cuthbert said.

"Madelene's the one who should become a doctor," said Effy. "Aunt Ada wanted me to go to college first to discover my one true purpose."

"Goose, a girl can't become a doctor." Sofia, the girl on the train, stepped from behind the big maple tree. She shook her head. "You will never cease to amaze me, Effy Rimaldi. I knew I'd spotted you in that circus wagon, standing beside that handsome boy. Please tell me you ran away to marry a trapeze artist."

Effy choked out a "no." She stood, brushed off the dried leaves that had stuck to her pinafore, then broke into a run toward Sofia.

"Friends do not leave friends standing at the train station without as much as a note." Sofia placed her hands on her hips. "Not to mention, I was swooning with worry, wondering where you'd run off."

As usual, Sofia always had more than enough words for both of them—which was a good thing, given Effy's current situation.

Sofia dropped her arms, broke into a smile, and hugged Effy. "But I forgive you."

Effy hugged Sofia back as if she was her only friend in the world—which, of course, she was. "What will your mother say when she discovers I'm a child of the circus?"

"Leave Mama to me, goose," said Sofia. "Right now, she thinks I'm with my governess, who thinks I'm with Mama. But why aren't you at the academy?"

Effy hung her head. "I don't know if I'll ever convince Phineas to send me."

Sofia gave Effy's hand a gentle squeeze. "Fathers can't say no to their daughters."

Perhaps not all fathers, but mine has no trouble at all, thought Effy.

Balally squeaked and chirped, eager to join in the conversation.

"Oh, my goodness," Sofia stepped back, her arm loosely draped around Effy's shoulders. "There are no words," she added breathlessly.

"Beautiful," offered Cuthbert, "majestic, intelligent, gentle ..."

"Cuthbert's partial to Balally," said Effy with a smile. "But he's correct."

"May I ... pet her?" Sofia asked. She was beginning to amaze Effy.

Sofia looked at Balally. With the softest of whispers, Sofia cooed at the gigantic beast. When Balally lowered her head, Sofia approached without hesitation and scratched behind the elephant's ear.

"My elephant has made another good friend," said Cuthbert. As he led Balally onto the path, Effy and Sofia fell in behind.

"Just so you know," Effy felt compelled to mention, "women can and have become doctors."

"Do you suppose there are husbands out there who don't mind wives with ambitions?" asked Sofia.

"I imagine Dr. Stowe's husband didn't mind, or her daughter's husband," Effy said, matter-of-factly. "Besides, women must be able to care for themselves and not be rescued like the princesses in your fairy tales."

Effy knew she was parroting Aunt Ada's lectures. It didn't matter. Her own heart agreed.

Sofia nodded. "I'm beginning to understand that no one is coming to our rescue. Mama must start her own business."

When they reached the circus grounds, Effy and Sofia froze.

Standing near the pen with their arms folded and huge scowls plastered on their faces were the ringmaster and Mrs. Winterbottom.

Sofia gasped and Effy's heart began to pound.

CHAPTER EIGHTEEN
AN ELEPHANT'S DILEMMA

Cuthbert slowed. He stopped Balally and patted her trunk. Looking at Effy and Sofia, he said in a quavering voice, "I fear we've made the ringmaster angry. Already, Phineas keeps talking about auctioning her off to local farmers."

Sofia let out a shriek. Her mother shot a sharp look her way, but Sofia ignored her. "Cuthbert, this he must *never* do. Reading the book, *Black Beauty*, showed me how cruelly we treat our animals. Why, it was in the newspaper that boys in the next town kept shooting one of those elephants sold to a farmer. They thought their stupid bullets couldn't pierce her hide."

"Sofia, come here now," Mrs. Winterbottom said forcefully.

"That elephant suffered most miserably before she died," Sofia hissed. "Those boys acted like she didn't feel pain or fear." Tears rolled down her cheeks, and not because her mother looked furious, or at least, in Effy's estimate, not entirely.

"Ephemia Rimaldi," the ringmaster said coldly. "A word, please. Do you think strolling with an elephant is what I meant by staying safe?" Phineas dropped his arms by his side, clenching and unclenching his fists.

Phineas sounded genuinely curious, but Effy knew his flashing eyes meant there was a storm of anger brewing.

"Balally's gentle and wise and smart," Effy tried to reassure him.

"You know nothing of beasts," growled Phineas. "Circus hands are killed every day by elephants that go rogue."

"Balally is not a rogue elephant. If you understood elephants, you'd realize only male elephants ..."

"Stop right there!" Phineas held his hand in front of Effy's face, and her words died on her lips.

Her so-called poppa did not appear to be fond of lengthy explanations. Phineas's glare held her transfixed for several seconds. Then he bellowed, "Tarnation, child, are you always so vexing!?"

Effy almost jumped out of her boots. She shook her head. "No ... I just ... I—"

Phineas cut her off. "I told you to stay out of danger."

"But I wasn't in danger ... I ..." Effy's words failed her. This was a rare thing, indeed.

Phineas lifted his arm and pointed his finger at Cuthbert. "You, get your elephant safely chained and penned." Cuthbert scrambled away with Balally.

"But ..." began Effy.

"You!" Phineas pointed to her caravan. "Get inside your wagon and stay there. Do not leave it until *I* say so."

Effy decided a hasty retreat would be for the best. She waved a hurried goodbye to Sofia.

This was a setback, truly, but Effy knew she must forge ahead. Aunt Ada would have said so.

The dinner gong sounded. Surely Phineas had not meant for her to starve to death inside a dark and creepy caravan. He must have meant she could leave for meals.

Effy shot out of her wagon and allowed herself a small detour. She headed straight for the elephant pen. "Cuthbert?"

"I'm up here." Cuthbert was perched on a tree branch overhanging the elephant's pen. He broke off a smaller branch and tossed it to Balally.

Balally lunged for the branch and began gnawing on its bark and leaves.

"Wouldn't she rather eat hay?" asked Effy. Bark didn't sound like a delicious dinner. Although ... hay didn't sound much better.

Effy reached into the pocket of her pinafore. Producing her last apple, she handed it to Balally.

Balally used her trunk to delicately pluck the apple from Effy's hand, and she swore Balally trilled: "Thank you."

Cuthbert climbed down from the tree. "Balally needs the bark and leaves to keep her teeth healthy." He said this flatly, and when he looked at Effy, she was surprised at his grim expression.

"What's wrong?" she asked.

Cuthbert began patting Balally's trunk as if he was soothing himself, not her. He looked back at Effy and took a breath. "I fear the ringmaster meant what he said. He will auction off Balally."

"No!"

Effy spun around and discovered Madelene was standing right behind her. She must have come to check on her patient. Madelene's face had gone pale as milk.

"Cuthbert, the ringmaster can't do that!" Madelene cried. Cuthbert used his sleeve to swipe his face.

Madelene grabbed Effy by the shoulders. "You must stop your father from selling off our elephant. I've seen so many circus elephants suffer because of unskilled caretakers. Make yourself useful, ringmaster's daughter. Save Balally."

Effy tried tamping down her temper but gave up. "How am I supposed to convince Phineas of anything? He just wants me out of his sight. You and your brother had a good part in that."

Madelene looked balefully at Balally. "Please, convince your father."

"My fate is sealed with Phineas," said Effy. "You heard him. I'm a step away from being sent to a boarding house."

"Then you must think of another way, for Balally's sake." Madelene hurried away.

How could she win the ringmaster's affection? Phineas had been very clear on two things: He thought Balally was a menace, and Effy could not be a performer, any more than he could be a father.

Madelene was right. Effy needed a new solution. Not just because Madelene had challenged her; Effy wasn't one to back away. This was ... something new. At this moment, she didn't care a fig what Madelene or anyone thought about her. She didn't even care about getting into a good school.

Balally mattered more.

CHAPTER NINETEEN

THE SAPPHIRE IS CURSED

Cuthbert held a branch as Balally's trunk curled around it. The elephant crunched it into her mouth while leaves and twigs scattered on the ground like breadcrumbs. Effy stood outside the pen, remembering a conversation she'd overheard a few nights before. It was important. Something about how Cuthbert could save his elephant.

The sapphire!

"Please forgive me," said Effy. "I didn't mean to eavesdrop between you and your uncle the other night, but don't you have a valuable gem you could sell, and send Balally back to Ceylon?"

"I need Balally's papers of ownership," said Cuthbert. "You can't just send a random elephant away on a boat." Then he sighed. "Besides, that sapphire is cursed. Calamity will strike any man who profits from it."

"Why does everyone believe in superstitions?" Effy placed her hands on her hips.

It wasn't just Cuthbert or his uncle.

"Stepping under a ladder will only bring bad luck to a tent rigger if a bucket falls on his head. Sofia didn't make friends with me because she found a hairpin on the train. And dear Aunt Ada didn't die because a bird crashed into her window." Effy fought back a few treacherous tears.

"You can't let a foolish belief cloud your judgements." Effy worried she was sounding uppity again, but she had to say it. "Curses aren't real."

"They are to my uncle." Cuthbert shoved his hands deep into the pockets of his billowing trousers. "And he's the one we must convince. I mean, as well as the ringmaster, to have a change of heart about signing away his elephant." He shook his head. "These are impossible tasks."

Silently, they walked across the sawdust-strewn midway toward the cook's tent. Coloured lanterns hung from poles and carts and glowed otherworldly in the dusky evening. They passed a vending cart cluttered with toy monkeys dangling on strings above a row of kewpie dolls. A carnival game of pins and balls stretched across the midway.

Effy's stomach grumbled as she passed a red cart piled with sacks of chestnuts ready for roasting. Another vending cart set on silver sunburst wheels was outfitted with a round tin pan for spinning sugar. She imagined sweet cotton candy melting on her tongue.

She'd only eaten apples all day. No wonder there was a dull thudding in her skull. Her mouth filled with saliva when they entered the cook's tent that once again smelled of cornbread and molasses.

"Beans, that's what we get for lunch and dinner every night. I heard Ringling Circus feeds its workers fried chicken," growled the strong man.

"Chicken?" Another handler spat on the ground in disgust. "I'd settle for a scrap of rabbit or pigeon meat in a stew. We haven't had the likes of any of that for a donkey's age."

Cuthbert and Effy held out tin plates as the cook scooped baked beans and tossed a huge hunk of warm cornbread on top. They sat on stools beside the trestle table, and Effy dived into her food with wolfish bites. A fly scurried across Effy's cornbread. "Get your own dinner," she mumbled with her mouth full, and flicked it with her finger.

As Effy watched the fly zigzag away, she noticed not everyone else in the cook's tent was miserable. Her eyes widened when she spotted Mr. Jefferson and

Miss Mabel sitting across from each other and gazing into each other's eyes. They were positively moonfaced. Between them sat a vase stuffed with a huge bunch of red carnations. Then Miss Mabel reached over and took Mr. Jefferson's hand.

Miss Dot stopped by Effy's table and whispered in her ear. "There's a rumour about a spring wedding. I also heard there's a certain ringmaster's daughter to whom they are beholden."

A grin spread across Effy's face. She remembered the rocks she'd tossed into the pond and how, from her single rock, a series of rings spread wider and wider. This felt the same.

"Phineas Rimaldi has summoned you."

Effy looked up at the heavily moustached man leaning over her. He was the canvas-man who rigged the tent. "You'd best leave the rest of your supper. Daughter or not, when the ringmaster summons, you go."

Effy felt her grin slide away. She pushed out her stool, exchanged a worried glance with Cuthbert, and quickly followed the man.

As Effy rushed to keep up, he barked orders at circus troupers who were making last-minute preparations for the show and setting up ticket booths.

The tiny mirrors decorating Phineas's caravan glowed orange in the setting sun. Effy stood on the step and knocked on the red door. Only then, did the boss canvas-man leave. She knocked again.

"Do not lollygag. Just come in," Phineas said gruffly.

Effy swallowed and slowly opened the door. Surprisingly, the interior of the caravan was spare and humble. No mirrors or paint decorated the pine walls, and it was furnished with a single cot built into the back. A heavy metal cashbox sat on the shelf. The only other stick of furniture was a small table on the other side of the wagon beside the sleeping cot. On that table sat a hurricane lamp, the wick glowing softly in the dim light, illuminating a circus ledger.

Phineas Rimaldi sat on his cot and hunched over the ledger, pouring over numbers. He wore a gold silk vest and had a chain dangling from his vest pocket. A white rabbit's foot was fastened to it.

For good luck, thought Effy. He's as superstitious as Aunt Ada and the other Rimaldis. Poor little rabbit, she couldn't help thinking.

Phineas squinted at the pages. "Profit," he mumbled. "This circus needs to make a bigger profit. Maybe if I held on longer to their wages, the interest rate will rise. And that elephant is operating at a loss. We only have tonight's and tomorrow's performance. So far, the elephant has eaten more than ticket sales."

Phineas scratched his neck. "We need ... we need to think of another attraction instead of that large beast. In fact, we need a new form of entertainment that doesn't have such a high overhead."

Effy cleared her throat. Phineas spun around. "Consternation! You're not Jefferson."

"I was told you summoned me."

Phineas gave his head a slight shake. *As if he's trying to shake the very thought of me loose,* Effy decided.

"Only because when I'd sent a plate of food to your caravan, you were not there. Vexation, child, what did I tell you. Stay in your wagon."

Not one to beat around the bush, Effy burst out with, "Don't sell Cuthbert's elephant." She would beg, if need be.

Phineas rose and took a step toward her. "You came here to be lectured to, not the other way around. This circus is *my* business. I don't want to hear one more word about elephants or anything else from you."

"Please don't sell Cuthbert's elephant," she begged.

Phineas slammed his fist on the table. The hurricane lamp teetered, and he had to quickly set the tipping glass shade upright. "What did I say? Spare me your caterwauling about that elephant."

Effy opened her mouth to speak, but Phineas shouted first.

"And I don't want to hear another word about your ambition to swing from a trapeze. One more word on either subject and I will whip you soundly."

Effy's eyebrows shot up. Even her mother's people, strict and grim as they were, did not resort to whippings. She bit her lip but refused back away.

Phineas's eyes softened for a moment, but he waved his arm. "Go to your wagon. Mark me—I need no more trouble from you. If we don't see a profit soon, we will lose our shirts and be sent to the poorhouse. That's a bottom fact. The elephant must be sold. Have enough wherewithal to see that *business* comes before friends, before *everything*."

Effy wanted to tell him how that was not true. *Lots* of things were more important than money. Balally, for one.

The circus hostler hovered at the door.

"You are needed in the stables. A horse has gone lame."

"Of course it has," complained Phineas. Without a backward glance, he brushed past Effy.

Effy was about to leave, and that was the truth, but

she decided she'd glance at the circus ledger. *Perhaps Phineas has forgotten about adding in his compound interest,* she thought. *I'll just check to see if he's calculated interest over rate and time.* She'd learned from Aunt Ada how that would improve his profit.

Effy couldn't take her eyes off the ledger, even as she wished she could look away. She'd been mistaken. Phineas hadn't been adding numbers in his ledger.

The telegram sat on top of the open pages. She stared at the inkwell, at the pen, at the sheet of paper addressed to that walrus, Uncle Edgar. A cold draft snaked up her spine.

Edgar you old chiseler Stop
Forward me the trust fund Stop
Or I will release the hounds of hell Stop
Signed Phineas Rimaldi LEGAL guardian Stop

CHAPTER TWENTY

A MOST CUNNING PLAN

Effy wanted to burn the telegram in the flame of the hurricane lamp and stomp on its ashes. Instead, she clutched her hands to her heart and read the telegram one more time. The words took their time sinking in.

Effy knew Phineas Rimaldi didn't care a whit about her. She'd held out a flicker of hope because he'd kept her in his legal guardianship. She also held out hope that while he said he was no father, she might convince him otherwise. Except it was all here in black and white.

Effy meant only one thing to her scoundrel father—a source of money for the circus.

Phineas planned to keep her trust money for himself, just as her other relatives had meant to. She could almost live with that. What she couldn't bear was that Aunt Ada's dream was about to come to nothing.

Aunt Ada had held the hope that women could become equal. Girls could be educated and take their place in the world. This dream had been Effy's ...

... And Effy had failed. She'd failed everyone on all accounts.

She slowly made her way back to her caravan. When had her boots become so heavy? Why did her limbs ache so? She decided she'd allow her new friend a night of blissful sleep. In the morning she'd tell Cuthbert she would never win her flimflamming, so-called poppa's affection, and that Cuthbert and his uncle were going to lose their elephant.

Oh, Balally, Effy thought. Her heart squeezed tight.

Effy crawled under the blanket on her bunk as an autumn chill settled outside. The wagon hissed as wind snaked through the window gap and under the door. Effy lit the kerosene lamp beside her, and the tiny flame guttered in the darkening gloom. To ease her mind, Effy stuck her nose into her poetry book. Despite the poem giving her nightmares the previous night, she decided any horror in the "Ancient Mariner" would be preferable to the horrors of her day.

One line at the end of the poem shot through her heart like an arrow hitting its mark. "Bless all creatures great and small." Like Balally and the tiger, she thought. They mattered. We all matter.

In the story, when the mariner accepted this, the curse finally broke. The albatross fell off his neck, and he sailed home. Effy placed the slim volume of Samuel Taylor Coleridge down on her blanket.

"That might be the best poem ever written," Effy said out loud.

Inspired, a plan commenced in her mind and grew like compound interest. "After all," Effy said to the stuffed monkey, "there is still one performance left."

When Effy at last laid her head on the pillow, she slept soundly. No nightmares crept into her sleep this time. Her only bad moment occurred, just as it had each morning, in that space between sleep and wakening. That's when she forgot for a second that she wasn't in her own bedroom and living with Aunt Ada. But then she remembered her plan and bounced out of bed.

The breakfast gong sounded. No one brought her a plate of food, so Effy decided that it was unlikely Phineas expected her to stay in her wagon. It was unlikely that he remembered her at all.

She dressed quickly, shot out of her caravan, and raced along the midway. A current of excitement travelled through the circus. Tonight would be the grand finale. Even the birds chirped a little louder.

The air was sharp, and dew beaded on the awning of the striped big top. When Effy joined Cuthbert and Madelene under the breakfast tent, the scent of apple and pumpkin fritters filled the air.

"At least it's not beans," Madelene said, forking a slice of fritter. Cuthbert spooned a mouthful of apple sauce and nodded.

Effy grabbed her tin plate and sat across from them at the table. "I've figured a way to convince your uncle to sell the sapphire and rescue Balally."

Madelene looked puzzled but held her sharp tongue—for once.

"Then you are a magician," said Cuthbert. "I told you, there's a curse. It doesn't matter whether or not we believe in it. My uncle does."

Effy held up her hand. "You're right. A curse is always true if you believe in it, just as ..." Effy's gaze darted at Madam Vadoma, who hurried through her breakfast so she could meet with clients.

"Just as there are people who believe Madam Vadoma can speak to spirits. So, that's why they think they hear from their loved ones. It's their heart's desire."

"I do not see how that will make my uncle sell his sapphire," said Cuthbert between mouthfuls of fritter.

"Hear me out," said Effy. "I read a poem by a brilliant poet, Samuel Taylor Coleridge."

Madelene rolled her eyes.

Effy ignored her and continued. "The ancient mariner in the poem broke the curse when he cared about '... *all things both great and small.*' Beasts, too, not just men," Effy added for final clarity.

Madelene shrugged but Cuthbert slammed his fist on the table, almost knocking over Effy's cup of cider.

"My uncle said the curse of the star sapphire was that no *man* can profit. If he sold the gem, *he* wouldn't profit, Balally would. That's the way my uncle could break the curse."

Effy nodded. "Because Balally's not a man, she's an elepha ..."

Madelene held up her hand. "I'm not daft; I get it now. Save the beast and break the curse." Then she turned to Cuthbert. "I didn't know you had a star sapphire. Those are very valuable. Do you think you can convince your uncle that he'll break the curse?"

Cuthbert rubbed his temples. When he smiled and looked back up, his expression sent hope flushing though Effy.

"He might," said Cuthbert. "It is his heart's desire to save Balally and retire to Ceylon."

Then a cloud passed over Cuthbert's sunny smile. "We still need Phineas to give us Balally's paper of ownership. How do we convince him not to auction her to the highest bidder? There might not be enough time to sell the sapphire, and even then, we won't have enough money to buy her back and book three passages to Ceylon."

"Did I hear you say you want to sell a sapphire?" Mr. Jefferson scraped his stool closer and leaned forward. "A widow is selling off her estate jewellery, so there's a jeweller in town. That's how I bought this." He winked and called Miss Mabel to the table.

Miss Mabel waltzed over as if she was waltzing down an aisle. She flashed a ring right under Effy's nose. The gold band held six tiny gemstones. With a graceful finger, Miss Mabel pointed to each gem. "Ruby, emerald, garnet, amethyst, ruby, diamond—that spells out *regard*." She beamed.

Mr. Jefferson cleared his throat and, with a twinge of embarrassment, said, "Effy, thank you."

Effy grinned. "Congratulations."

Mr. Jefferson stood and took Miss Mabel's hand. Then they wandered out of the cook tent, oblivious to anyone else.

"You leave Phineas to me," Effy said to Cuthbert. "I have another circus performance planned. You work on your uncle." After Cuthbert raced away, Effy turned to Madelene.

"Oh, no, you don't," said Madelene. "I want to help, truly, but I cannot convince Mama to let you swing from the trapeze. She won't allow it. You have to find another way to worm into the ringmaster's black heart. Try convincing one of the clowns to let you join them."

Effy doubted wearing floppy shoes and throwing popped corn into the audience would convince Phineas she was a worthy performer. She needed to think up a much more amazing act, so in turn, he'd be convinced he could be a better poppa. She left Madelene and walked toward the clown tent. She spotted a man in white face paint, pushing a large wooden bicycle.

"Is that bicycle part of your circus act?" asked Effy.

"What's a bicycle?" the clown asked as he pushed the bicycle. The pedals pumped in the air as if a ghost rode it.

"... That's a bicycle," said Effy, wondering if he was joking.

The man leaned the big wooden two-wheeler against the tent canvas. His giant lips twitched into what might have been a smile ... or a frown. It was hard to tell under the paint.

"This is a velocipede; I call it a waste of money."
He shrugged his shoulders. "The ringmaster paid a lot
of coin for this newfangled invention. Money he could
have used to buy meat for our suppers. He thought I
could ride it around and entertain the audience. Only I
don't know how to ride this devil's contraption."

"I can," Effy piped up.

"You can what?" The clown's lips twitched again.

"Ride the bicycle," Effie smiled. He used the same
old-fashioned word for it as Aunt Ada. "I mean ... the
velocip ..."

"Girls can't ride velocipedes," he laughed.

"Of course, they can," Effy shot back. "If I take this
devil's contraption off your hands, could you put me in
tonight's show to ride in your place?"

"Consider it done." The clown handed over the
bicycle, and with a short bow, retreated into the tent.

Effy recalled when she'd first seen such a riding
contraption. She'd discovered one in her aunt's carriage
house. When she'd showed Aunt Ada, a wistful smile
had spread across her aunt's face.

"It was once my heart's desire to ride that thing,"
Aunt Ada had said. "I believed riding about on a bicycle
was a sure way to set a woman free."

Effy had lifted the wooden bicycle from the wall. She remembered telling her aunt, "It's heavy, and the wheels are so large, and the seat is so high off the ground. How did you manage?"

"I didn't. I fell and gave it up at once." Aunt Ada had looked rueful. "How would me breaking my neck serve the suffragists?" She'd winked at Effy. "It's up to some daring younger girl."

Effy took her aunt up on that challenge. After a few bloody knees and badly bruised elbows, she'd conquered the contraption.

Effy pushed the velocipede away from the clown's tent. She'd never actually ridden a bicycle beyond Aunt Ada's carriage house, so she spent the rest of the morning practising in a field behind the woods.

✳

After a lunch of cold fritters, Effy retreated to her caravan. Reaching under her bunk, she took out her embroidered bag. Tugging out her prized green dress, she took the pair of scissors she'd not yet returned to Miss Mabel and began snipping.

It did not hurt her heart a whit to shorten the dress until it fell just below her knees. The silk wasn't holding up well in circus life, anyway. She cut pale green strips from the discarded end of her skirt and took out her embroidery kit.

Effy threaded her needle and sewed a tight green cuff on the end of each leg of her frilliest, best, pantaloons. Next, Effy took out her gold suffragist sash, and sewed on the final leftover patches of green silk.

She embroidered the sash until her fingers ached.

"Let the show begin," she declared to the stuffed monkey on the shelf.

CHAPTER TWENTY-ONE

A TRUE CALAMITY

A massive flock of birds flew across the sky and blacked out the setting sun. When the raucous bird calls faded, the townspeople came. Effy waited near the caravans and watched their approach. The townsfolk carried lanterns in a ghostly procession, winding down the grass-trampled trail and through the carnival grounds.

Farmers with bent backs, their faces and hands wizened with hard work, had donned clean shirts and straw hats. Stoop-shouldered women in plain brown dresses wore bonnets on their heads, shading their creased faces. Boys wore woollen shirts and belted trousers, and girls had on dark dresses that fell to their ankles, their hair tightly braided and pinned under their bonnets.

Everyone's face wore an expectant look, and a thirst for adventure shone in their eyes. Effy wondered why she'd ever thought circuses didn't matter.

As the townsfolk purchased their tickets and entered

the tent, Effy slipped from the caravan rows and made her own way into the big top. She hovered at the back in clown alley.

The steam calliope pumped out a trilling racket as Effy paced outside the performers' entrance. Worry gnawed her stomach. Inside the big top, she heard Balally trumpet and the audience gasp. Someone was shouting. Effy lifted the tent flap and peered inside. Things weren't going well for Cuthbert.

Balally arced her trunk and stomped her very large elephant foot. Sawdust flew as Balally trumpeted again. The crowd roared in fear. Cuthbert tried settling Balally, and then he tried hushing the audience. No one listened to him.

"Please, girl, stand," Cuthbert commanded. Instead, Balally stepped off the giant balancing stool and trotted toward the audience. Effy thought she took dainty footsteps for an elephant. The audience disagreed.

Balally stepped over the ring and leaned into the audience. As people shrieked and fled the front row, the elephant helped herself to spilled popcorn. Phineas, dressed in his ringmaster tailcoat and top hat, shouted, "Rein in your elephant!"

"Balally, come back." Cuthbert tugged his elephant's lead.

When Balally ignored Cuthbert, Phineas walked over and snapped his whip beside Balally's bandaged leg. Effy gasped as Balally slammed her trunk down and knocked off the ringmaster's hat. Phineas double-stepped backward and almost toppled over.

Nervous laughter rattled around the audience. They weren't sure if this was part of the act. Cuthbert's uncle flew from the shadows, holding his hand to his chest. Effy could hear his harsh breathing. In gasps, the uncle coaxed Balally from the ring.

Effy felt a tap on her shoulder and turned around. Madelene had broken away from the Great Yolandas and whispered, "Cuthbert's uncle was too sick again to perform. Cuthbert's not himself, either. Balally knows something's wrong. That's why she's acting up."

"Do you think Cuthbert couldn't convince his uncle to sell the sapphire?" Worry tugged Effy's heart.

Madelene tilted her head then shrugged. "The way they were behaving before the show, it was as if disaster had already hit them both."

Phineas, Effy thought. Had he already told them he was selling off Balally? Now she needed this performance more than ever. She had to win over that scoundrel's heart—for all their sakes.

"By the way," said Madelene, gazing at Effy. "That's, ah, quite an interesting costume." Effy thought so, too. The shorter dress and decorated pantaloons had turned out even better than she'd hoped.

Madelene raised her eyebrows when she spotted the bicycle. "You know how to perform tricks on a bicycle?"

Tricks? It hadn't occurred to Effy that she'd be doing more than riding the bicycle in circles and showing off her important message. Effy was about to ask Madelene what sort of tricks.

"We're on," shouted Jacque. Madelene quickly joined her family, and the Great Yolandas entered the circus arena.

Phineas promised, if the audience remained in their seats, that the next astounding act wouldn't frighten the ladies. Effy scoffed. She'd seen more than a few *men* scramble from their seats when Balally stepped outside the ring.

"The next acts of derring-do will leave you spellbound with amazement. Behold the greatest show on Earth!" Phineas shouted. Then he did an odd thing. He went behind the steam calliope and spun around three times before the Yolandas stepped into the ring. Effy had never noticed that before.

"Why did he do that?" Effy asked to no one in particular.

A clown shot her a puzzled look. "What? Turn around like that? We've been having our circus troubles. Phineas did that to get rid of bad luck." He lifted the tent flap higher and went inside.

Effy shook her head. She must have got her practical mind from her mother. She held the flap open and watched the Great Yolandas. When Madelene swung on the trapeze and leapt from the arms of Yolanda and into the outstretched arms of Jacque, Effy's jaw dropped. Then Jacque swung and changed swings. Both were no match for the Great Yolanda, who somersaulted twice in mid-air before catching the swing that Madelene passed her.

Next, male and female acrobats did tumbles and cartwheels across the sawdust floor. One boy balanced on a ball as his sister tumbled round and round inside a hoop. In the next act, a man and a woman stood on their feather-plumed horses as they circled the ring. In every act, the women's abilities and courage matched the men's.

The tiger tamer then outmatched the courage of any man. She held out fiery hoops as her tiger jumped through them.

Doesn't the audience see women should be allowed to do anything? Then Effy's next thought was how her idea, which had seemed brilliant in the morning, had dimmed. She was no match for these performers.

"Are you actually riding that bicycle?" a gentle voice asked.

Effy turned and faced Cuthbert. Her friend looked grim.

"You *do* say girls can do anything. I believe you will impress Phineas," he mumbled.

After witnessing the other circus acts, Effy was half-ready to flee. Then Cuthbert's face crumpled. "Only, I fear it will not help Balally."

"Cuthbert, I will do my best," she managed to croak, even though her knees had started wobbling. "I know it's only riding a bicycle, but I will make it count."

"You will amaze the audience. Only, I meant that it doesn't matter for *us* anymore," said Cuthbert. "The sapphire has been stolen."

Effy's stomach dropped. "No! What? Are you sure? How?"

"I spent the afternoon convincing my uncle that we could break the curse if we sold the sapphire to save Balally. As you said, a beast would profit, not a man. And ... my uncle believed that might be so."

"Only I was a fool." Cuthbert buried his face in his hands.

"What do you mean?" Effy asked.

"My uncle went into our tent and brought the sapphire out. He unwrapped the ring from the silk cloth and held it up in the sunlight. The star in the middle of the blue gem shone in bright, clean lines. The sapphire showed its value."

Cuthbert struggled over his next words. "He handed me the sapphire, Effy, and bid me to take it into town right away, in case the jeweller was fixing to leave. My uncle trusted me. But I left the ring on the stool beside Balally while I grabbed my bag. I left for only a moment, thinking no one would go into her pen. When I came out, the sapphire was gone. I think it is truly cursed."

A cold finger of dread trailed down Effy's back, but she shook it off. "What if Balally bumped into the stool and the ring rolled off."

"I searched the pen. I even," Cuthbert grimaced, "checked the dung."

That was desperate, indeed.

The band inside the tent stopped playing their marching tune, and a horn trumpeted. The clown who'd given Effy the velocipede stuck his head out of the tent flap. He squeezed his big red rubber nose and said, "Are you ready for your performance?"

Effy gulped and looked under the flap. Phineas's voice rang out. "Ladies and gentlemen, get ready for our next aamaaazing act!" Once more he stepped behind the calliope and spun three times.

The clown lifted the flap higher and waved Effy inside.

CHAPTER TWENTY-TWO

THE DARING YOUNG GIRL ON THE FLYING BICYCLE

"I'll help search for the sapphire as soon as I'm done here," Effy told Cuthbert. The sapphire had to be somewhere nearby. Cuthbert was right. No one would dare climb inside the elephant pen and steal it. Balally would say something—in elephant language, of course.

Effy took her gold and green sash and draped it over her shoulders. Then she grabbed the bicycle. It felt far heavier than when she'd practised with it that afternoon. Also, her hands ached from all her embroidery, but she managed to grip the handlebars and scramble onto the seat.

Effy pushed forward. She struggled to keep her balance on the sawdust. After a few more wobbly pushes on the pedals, she rode the velocipede straight into the tent. Mindful of Phineas's threat that she must never again step inside a circus ring, Effy rode *outside* the ring.

Effy rode past the clown who laughed and muttered, "Well, haven't you just bested me."

The band was playing, "The Man on the Flying Trapeze," but they looked in Effy's direction and faltered. The maestro whispered, "Make haste and switch to 'Ride of the Valkyries.'" A man crashed his cymbals, and the band began belting out the stormy tune.

Phineas Rimaldi shot Effy a look of pure fury, but then he announced, "Ladies and Gentlemen, behold ... ah ... behold our newest act!"

Effy circled a wobbly path between the circus ring and the audience. The wooden wheels turned slowly in the sawdust and kept pitching her forward. She struggled to keep riding. As she circled close to the audience, she heard gasps of "oohs" and "ahs."

Effy rode toward the circus performers who had gathered by the calliope. When they read the words on her sash, they clapped loudly.

"Here, here," bellowed the tall man.

"Yes!" yelled Miss Dot.

"Equality for all," the women performers shouted.

"Equal pay for us all!" yelled Yolanda and the tiger tamer. Soon, the rest of the women performers joined in, their voices roaring.

Effy had spent the afternoon embroidering on one side of her sash: **Equal Rights.** On the other side she'd written: **For Everyone: Large and Small.**

When Effy circled the audience again, she overheard, "Sofia, look!"

Effy spotted Mrs. Winterbottom sitting stock straight on the closest bench, full of alertness. She grabbed her daughter's hand.

"I told you that Effy was brave and bold, Mama."

"Wouldn't it be wonderful to ride anywhere we wished," said Mrs. Winterbottom.

"Yes, Mama, it looks fun." Sofia waved then clapped.

Under the spotlight, Effy rode harder and pushed the bicycle faster, gaining momentum. The band built "Ride of the Valkyries" into a powerful crescendo as cymbals crashed. The drumbeat reverberated around the tent.

Effy decided she needed a flashy finish, something besides riding in circles. She spotted a ramp outside the ring that the acrobats used to launch into the air. She rode toward it.

Leaning forward, Effy stood and pushed harder on the pedals. The muscles in her legs protested, but she ignored the burn. Once the bicycle gained speed, the drums and cymbals built like a thunderstorm. Effy shot up the ramp.

She balanced on the block pedals, wrenched her

waist, and swiveled her hips to twist the bicycle. Her legs cramped and froze. The wooden bicycle tipped, and then it crashed.

Effy landed underneath the heavy contraption and watched fireworks behind her eyelids—shooting red rockets, yellow lightning bolts, and blue sapphires.

Then the lights went out for the second time in a week.

"She is waking up."

"She must be. She's been mumbling something about a cursed ring."

"Come on, dear, open your eyes."

Someone shook Effy's shoulder. Effy mumbled, "Coming Aunt Ada."

The wet cloth on Effy's forehead dribbled water down the back of her neck. She pulled off the cloth. Someone put it back.

"Effy, open your eyes."

Effy pushed up on her elbows, opened her eyes, and took in her surroundings. At first, she thought she was outside, but then she realized those weren't really stars. They were the veils that hung from Madam Vadoma's ceiling. Effy fell back on the bunk and gingerly rubbed the egg-sized lump on her head.

Miss Mabel sat on the edge of the bed and took Effy's hand. "Try a sip of this. It is Professor Tipillberry's Elixir from the medicine show. The label says it's just the tonic to get you up and around." Miss Mabel waved the foul-smelling brown bottle under Effy's nose.

Effy clamped her lips shut until Miss Mabel put the bottle down. "Probably for the best," the bearded lady muttered.

"Cook said you would come to, so this iz good, no?" Madam Vadoma sat on the chair beside the table. She nodded. "He also said nothing inside you was likely broken."

"The cook? I want Madelene's opinion. Or shouldn't you send for a doctor? That's what Aunt Ada would have done." Effy flexed her legs and arms. Everything *seemed* to work.

"We could send for a doctor, but our cook's set more broken bones than any quack." Miss Mabel shook her head. "Besides, a doctor would probably bleed you. Leeches sometimes make folk weaker."

"Don't send for the doctor. Forget I even mentioned it." Effy couldn't emphasize this enough, having once seen a leech.

"Is the circus show over?"

Madam Vadoma opened the caravan door a crack, and weak sunlight trickled inside. "You were out all night long. It's now a short while past sunrise."

"That was quite the performance," chuckled Miss Mabel. "The audience gave you a standing ovation."

Madame Vadoma scoffed. "Nothing excites the audience like almost killing a performer. We'd have a sold-out show tonight if we weren't closing."

Effy had won. She'd proven she could be a performer. Now Phineas had to act like a proper poppa. For a moment, she was puzzled why Phineas wasn't here. She'd been lying unconscious and likely near dead. Shouldn't he have stayed by her side?

Effy slid her legs out of the covers. She was still dressed in her performance costume. Madame Vadoma tsked and said, "No wonder you had a calamitous accident. A circus performer should never wear green. It's bad ..."

"Luck." Effy rolled her eyes as she swung her legs over the side of the bed.

"Effy, you stay put," ordered Miss Mabel.

But Effy *had* to find Cuthbert and search for that ring. Madame Vadoma whispered something to Miss Mabel, and they slipped out of the caravan. Miss Mabel frowned deeply and said over her shoulder, as she shut the door, "We'll check back soon."

There was something going on. And likely nothing good. Effy got out of bed and tested her shaky legs. When she stepped out of the caravan, birds chirped up a chorus. Effy perched on the top step of the wagon and stared across the carnival grounds.

The rising sun pinked up the sky, but black clouds were moving in. The air had the bite of a coming storm. She had not liked the expression on Miss Mabel's face.

Trouble was coming—Effy could feel it.

CHAPTER TWENTY-THREE
PARADIDDLES

Effy's stomach knotted when she heard Balally trumpet in distress. She flew off the last steps of the caravan, turned the corner sharply, and met up with the outstretched hand of Phineas Rimaldi.

"Whoa, stop right there. Child, you look worse than a sick cat in the rain. Turn yourself around and get straight back to bed."

"I'm feeling fine."

"Tarnation, girl, do I have to tell you twice." Phineas loomed over her.

"No *sir*, I do apologize," Effy said meekly. She cast her eyes down, turned around, and headed toward the caravan.

"Good girl." Phineas sounded surprised.

When Effy reached the front of the caravan, she zig-zagged around its other side, and weaved through the baggage wagons lined up in rows. Passing behind the cook tent, she made her way through the carnival grounds, past the rickety Ferris wheel and steam calliope. When she reached the striped big top, Effy doubled back toward the elephant pen.

Her heart sank and she almost crumpled. Her shoulders felt like she was carrying a giant sack of potatoes.

Cuthbert stood, his feet planted, his arms gesturing, while he argued with a group of men. Balally thrashed in her chains, trumpeting wildly.

The elephant's eyes were wide and wild; she flattened her ears against the side of her head as she tossed her head to and fro. She flailed her trunk at the growing crowd of gawking circus performers. Men scurried from her stomping feet as the workers tried loading her onto a huge, flat, straw-filled wagon. The team of horses hitched to the wagon stamped their hooves in growing agitation.

A couple of men had dragged Cuthbert's uncle away and pinned him against the front of the wagon. "Please, allow me to reassure my elephant. You are frightening her," urged Cuthbert's uncle.

One of the workers from town—a wiry man with a gigantic black moustache—said, "She aint *yer* elephant no more. We've got orders to ship her out on the train."

"The ringmaster is investigating a theft of ours, good

sirs," said Mr. Amal. "If we recover our treasure, we can afford the elephant's passage back to Ceylon. I beg you, sirs, talk to the ringmaster."

Cuthbert shouted for the townsmen to leave Balally alone. Tears were streaming down Miss Dot's face. Madame Vadoma and Miss Mabel had their arms around each other. Mr. Jefferson, who'd gone a shade of green, tore off his black cap and threw it on the ground.

But none of them stopped the men loading Balally onto the wagon.

A suspicion crept into Effy's mind. That scoundrel father of hers hadn't been concerned one whit about her health. When he'd ordered bed rest, he was keeping her from seeing this sorry spectacle. He knew Effy was dead set against him selling Balally.

Cuthbert threw himself between Balally and the townsmen trying to take her away. The man with the moustache swatted Cuthbert on the head.

"Hey!" shouted Mr. Jefferson. "There's no need for that."

Effy flew to her friend's side. Mr. Jefferson grabbed her arm and pulled her back. "Don't you get all worked up, Miss Effy. This is a sorry state, but it's circus business."

Effy broke away, ran forward, and planted herself in

front of the men struggling with Balally's chains. "I am the ringmaster's daughter!" she shouted. "And I've been sent to tell you the circus is **not** selling our elephant!"

The men stopped struggling and stood stock still. Confusion crossed their faces, though, truth be told, Effy thought most of them looked relieved. It was no easy task, loading a reluctant elephant onto a wagon.

Effy turned and faced the growing crowd. "Do you hear me? We're *not* selling Balally! The ringmaster changed his mind."

"Vexation, girl, what are you up to?" Phineas Rimaldi charged through the crowd. He didn't look happy.

The man with the handlebar moustache said, "The girl says you changed yer mind. Are you shipping this elephant off or not?"

Phineas's eyes flashed. "Enough of these paradiddles. I'll hear no more of your foolish talk, Ephemia."

"No. Do not sell Balally, you can't. I ... I forbid it."

A few of the performers gasped. Phineas stormed toward Effy, his eyes flashing. "Girl," he thundered, "if you hadn't already half-killed yourself on the velocipede, I'd ... I'd ..."

Effy took several steps backward and bumped into Madam Vadoma who put an arm around her shoulder.

Phineas sighed and turned to the men who'd come for Balally. "I told her no such thing. The elephant must go. This girl is still addle-brained from her accident on the velocipede."

Miss Mabel tsked and said, "That's true. Poor thing only just awoke, mumbling over and over in her delirium about curses."

Madam Vadoma nodded in agreement.

By this time, the whole circus had gathered by the elephant tent—the whole circus except for Madelene. Where was she? She would hardly miss this calamity.

The circus troupers looked to Phineas. Balally strained against her chains while Cuthbert shouted at them, "Back off and leave her be!"

"Is there any hope we can delay until our treasure is found?" Mr. Amal asked one more time.

"Business is business." Phineas said this slowly, weariness edging his voice. He turned his attention to the crowd. "I am sorry, but I have no choice."

People began grumbling. "This circus won't be worth a wooden nickel without an elephant," said the strong man.

Phineas said, "I will soon have more than enough money to pay all of you all your wages. And there will be a fifty dollar bonus per person."

"That's ... that's wonderful, no?" Madam Vadoma dropped her arm from Effy's shoulder. "I can leave the circus and start my own business. There's always a need for a talented fortune teller."

A change of mood swept through the crowd. All the circus performers broke into groups and began discussing their plans for spending their windfall. Miss Dot dried her tears. She squeezed Effy's hand, saying, "I think this might be the end of the road for us all."

Effy wasn't sure what she meant. How could it be the end for anyone but Balally? She swiped her own blurring eyes. When she swallowed, it burned down her throat. Did Miss Dot mean things couldn't get worse? Effy agreed with that.

Madelene emerged from the shadows behind the big top. She, her brother, and her mother were followed by a man in a navy policeman's uniform, sporting a tin badge on his chest.

"Phineas," said the constable. "These people right here are your thieves." The constable pushed Jacque in front of Phineas. "I've got a telegram from the last town saying that they have outstanding debts." Then he jabbed his finger at the Great Yolanda. "Also, this lady here is of a shady background."

"Did you find the ring?" Phineas said coolly.

"Well, no," said the constable.

Madelene's flushed face didn't stop her from holding Effy's gaze, almost daring her to say something. Then she said through gritted teeth, "We didn't steal anything."

"Mama injured herself in the last town, and we needed a doctor, not your bone-cracking cook," said Jacque. He spat on the ground. "We'll pay up our debt when you pay us, Phineas."

Yolanda straightened herself and lifted her chin in proud defiance. She crossed her arms and said, "We are not thieves."

"You heard her," Phineas told the constable.

The constable took off his helmet and scratched his head. "I only have one other suspect, and he's reported to be a man of good character. Only he spent quite a bit of money yesterday on an engagement ring—a Mr. Jefferson."

Effy's hand flew to her mouth. Cuthbert had said no one had known about the sapphire. That is, until she'd eavesdropped on Cuthbert and his uncle. Then she'd casually mentioned it in front of Madelene. Then Mr. Jefferson had advised them about the jeweller.

There were two sides to Madelene—one good, one

bad. And where did Mr. Jefferson get the money to buy Miss Mabel her ring? Phineas hadn't paid his workers their wages.

Effy shook her head. No. They wouldn't. In her excitement over her clever idea about the sapphire, lots of other people could have overheard her.

Only one person could be held responsible for this calamity. "Oh, Cuthbert," Effy whispered to herself. "I'm so sorry."

CHAPTER TWENTY-FOUR
ALL THE LIKELY SUSPECTS

Wind scuttled between the rows of carnival tents, making banners flap and leaves fly. Its eerie whistle announced the storm's arrival. A few drops of rain pitter-pattered on the trampled dirt near the elephant pen. A few more drops landed on Effy's aching head.

"Jefferson bought the engagement ring *before* the sapphire was missing," Phineas grumbled.

That was right, Effy thought in relief.

"I suppose," said the constable, rubbing his chin. "Well, then, that leaves me these three suspects."

"I don't believe they would have robbed another performer. We're a family here," said Phineas.

Effy thought he could have said the last part more convincingly, like he had when he vouched for Mr. Jefferson.

Madelene drew herself up. Jacque put his arm around her. Their mother stared down Phineas and the constable with a face that could have been carved from stone.

Phineas turned to Mr. Amal, who still looked beseechingly from Phineas to the Great Yolandas, hoping for a miracle for Balally.

"I would bear no ill will if my sapphire is returned," Mr. Amal said.

Jacque spat on the ground again. "It's the same wherever we go. We're considered bad characters because we have no father and move around. The circus tolerates us, but because we're carnival folk, the townspeople call us riffraff."

Aunt Ada would have said the Yolandas were riffraff. Effy's cheeks heated up because she would have believed her. No wonder Madelene had called Effy uppity. Maybe Aunt Ada hadn't been right about everything.

If Effy had learned one thing at the circus, it was that *everyone* needed to be listened to and respected, not just people in refined society. Madelene hung her head again until Yolanda said, "Well, they're all wrong. We are the Great Yolandas—aerialists extraordinaire—artists of derring-do. Not thieves."

"They wouldn't steal," said Effy. She knew Madelene wouldn't destroy Balally's only chance.

Mr. Amal turned back to Phineas. "Just give us a little more time," he said. "We need to find the sapphire."

"I cannot afford to feed this elephant for one more day," said Phineas. "I am sorry, but we have all run out of time."

Effy was confused. Hadn't Phineas told the circus workers he could pay them bonuses? She scrutinized his face. He looked cantankerous—like he always did.

Cuthbert's uncle hung his head as he calmed Balally, rubbing her trunk and whispering soft words. Then he led the elephant into the wagon. Cuthbert buried his face in his hands. All Effy could do was watch as the last hope of helping Balally slipped from her grasp.

The constable brought out a pair of handcuffs and snapped one cuff on Jacque's wrist, and the other cuff on Yolanda. "Your family is under arrest."

Madelene swiped her arm over her face, but no tears flowed. "Save Balally," she told Effy. "Find the ring."

Miss Mabel broke from the crowd of gawking performers and patted Madelene's arm. "There, there." The constable raised his eyebrows as he stared at her beard.

Madelene jerked her head in Effy's direction as she was led toward a buggy. "Hurry—for Balally's sake and ours."

"Ephemia must rest," declared Phineas. "She is terribly confused." Effy flinched when he brushed away the hair on top of her head.

"Look at this goose egg." He made sure everyone saw the lump, then added in a voice full of concern, "Back to bed, child."

How could Effy rest? This entire disaster was on account of her and her big mouth. The last of the lingering circus performers broke up, and they made their way back to their wagons. Only one or two mentioned how it was too bad about the Great Yolandas.

Grit and dust rose in tiny wind tornadoes and pricked Effy's face. She stood frozen to the ground as the hostlers and townsmen chained Balally in the wagon. Cuthbert jumped in the wagon alongside his uncle. He turned to Effy and shouted, "I'll try and stop them from loading Balally on the train."

The wagon pulled away, blurring in Effy's tears. She ran after it.

Choking on dust, and dodging rock spray, she shouted, "Cuthbert! Don't leave. Help me search for the ring." She swallowed a mouthful of grit.

Cuthbert leaned over the wagon and shouted back, "Effy, I have to try and help Balally first. I can't let her get on that train. It's up to you to find the ring."

"How?" Effy cried. The wagon lumbered and rolled toward the station.

The constable secured the Great Yolandas in a small black buggy with wire-spoke wheels. He cracked his whip and shook the horse reins.

"Where are you taking them?" Effy called out.

"These outlaws will be biding their time in jail until the courthouse opens." The horse began trotting. The buggy disappeared into the dust clouds.

Not since Aunt Ada died, had Effy felt so alone.

"Ephemia for the last time—confine yourself to your bed." Phineas placed a hand on Effy's shoulder. Effy nodded, feeling as weary as a chicken who'd been terrorized the livelong night by a fox. But as soon as Phineas turned and stepped away, Effy headed in the opposite direction of her caravan, toward the grass field outside the elephant pen.

Dark clouds had rolled in and covered the sky. Tall field grass swayed and bent under shrieking wind. Effy knew it wasn't possible for the sapphire ring to roll off the stool, out of the pen, and into the grass field this far away. She had to look anyway. She stooped down and scrutinized the ground, then got down on her hands and knees and searched every blade of damp grass, as several fat raindrops plopped on her head. She backtracked and climbed inside the empty elephant pen. Finally, she crawled through sawdust underneath every single circus wagon that sat close to the animal menagerie—in case the ring had rolled under one of them.

The hours ticked by. The train would leave the station soon, with Balally on it.

Effy's skull ached, her back ached, and her heart ached. She slid down beside a wagon wheel and sat on the hard ground. Her lacy pantaloons were torn at both knees. Grease stains and dirt striped her meadow-green dress, and one sniff told her she smelled worse than Balally's elephant pen.

If only she could bury herself under the mound of leaves that were piled at the edge of the woods. She'd sleep for a hundred and fifty years, like Rip Van Winkle. Then, when she awoke, all her problems would be gone. It would be a whole new world, and maybe she wouldn't need to fight so hard.

Since when do problems disappear when you're like an ostrich burying your head in the sand—that's what Aunt Ada would have said.

"What would you do now, Aunt Ada?" Effy asked, with her face turned to the sky. In her heart, she believed Aunt Ada would want to help Balally and the Yolandas, circus folk or not.

Crows flew through the sky and hid in the trees, calling their flock to find shelter in the coming storm. One crow landed on a fencepost of the elephant pen: One is for sorrow; a second crow landed beside it: two is for joy; a third, fourth, fifth, and finally, a sixth crow lined the fence.

"Do you know where the sapphire ring is?" Effy asked the nearest crow. She shook her head. "No, I didn't think so." Counting crows, cursed sapphires, wearing green, turning three times to rid one's self of bad luck—what if it wasn't nonsense? Even Aunt Ada had been superstitious.

But Aunt Ada hadn't been right about everything.

Effy stood up and picked out a large piece of sawdust digging into her stocking. Locking the rows of circus caravans in her gaze, she went over her list of possible suspects again. Madelene hadn't stolen the ring—she meant what she said when she declared she was no thief. Besides, she cared too much about Balally.

Mr. Jefferson had bought the engagement ring *before* he'd overheard her talking about the sapphire. That's what Phineas had said.

Wait.

Phineas?!

CHAPTER TWENTY-FIVE

THE RINGMASTER'S SECRET

Where was Phineas Rimaldi getting all that money to pay off the circus performers *and* give them a fifty dollar bonus? He'd already arranged to ship out Balally because he said he couldn't afford to feed her.

So how had Phineas come into his so-called sudden windfall? Even selling Balally wouldn't cover all the costs.

Her trust fund would take time while it went through the courts. Besides, his telegram to Uncle Edgar wouldn't even have arrived yet. Telegrams might travel in seconds, but as Effy found out, it takes a might longer to deliver them.

What if her own father had heard that Mr. Amal owned a valuable ring? What if he saw the dazzling sapphire shining on the stool when he strolled by. At this very moment, the sapphire could be hidden somewhere inside Phineas's caravan.

Effy was suddenly sure of it. Only, she couldn't

exactly knock on the door and politely ask Phineas to step outside while she searched for the ring.

Picking up a broken tree branch, Effy stomped toward the most gaudily painted caravan in the circus, the one decorated with gold lettering and mirrors; it had trapeze artists painted on one side, and an elephant painted on the other. Effy stuck the tree branch in the spokes of the wagon wheel and rattled it, making a racket, betting Phineas wouldn't appreciate his daughter creating such a display.

As people poked their heads out caravan doors, Effy shouted, "Violets are blue, roses are yellow, and Phineas Rimaldi is a dishonest fellow." She shouted this while circling the wagon and banging the wheels—clack, clack, clickety-clack.

"He's promised you money and meat for the cook, but you'll get not a penny because he's a crook."

The crowd started grumbling. "Is the ringmaster's daughter completely addled?"

"She's as sharp as they come," said Miss Dot. "I've a mind Phineas is up to something."

"Tarnation," Phineas slammed open the door of his caravan. "You've vexed me for the last time, Ephemia."

The crowd quickly disappeared behind their

slamming doors. Effy ducked behind the caravan in the next row, just before Phineas stepped into view.

"Hiding won't help you, girl. You are a viper in my nest, and I shall root you out." He headed Effy's way, so she shot behind the next caravan, then the next, until she'd woven her way back to the ringmaster's wagon.

In his haste, Phineas had left his door flapping in the blustery wind. Effy stepped inside his caravan. A gust of wind rattled the shutters, and she heard a clap of thunder. A dart of panic shot through her heart. The sun would set soon. Where would Phineas stash a ring? She lifted his circus ledger, then rifled through his papers. If only her head didn't throb.

Then she spotted a familiar object on his shelf. Of course. His cash box! Heading for the shelf where the shiny metal cash register sat, sweat made Effy's hands greasy. They kept sliding off the raised number keys. She wiped her hands against her grimy dress. Then she tried again.

"Please open," she begged. She pressed the release key and heard a click and snap. A drawer popped out, but there was no sapphire's glow inside the shadowy drawer.

"I see," said a voice behind her. Effy spun around.

"You tell me money isn't everything," said Phineas. "But here you are helping yourself to mine."

"There is no money inside," Effy said unabashed. "It's as empty as a bird's nest in winter."

"Phineas." She couldn't say Poppa; the word stuck in her throat. "Please. You can save Balally and help Madelene."

"Phineas is it? You speak as if we're equals." He spoke in a tone so icy, Effy's heart plummeted to her scuffed boots. He took a small step toward her. Effy pressed against the shelf. He took another step forward.

"The sapphire may be worth a fortune, but a larger fortune you will lose," Effy warned him.

Phineas, like all the Rimaldis, was superstitious. Effy would fight fire with fire. "The sapphire is cursed," she said. "I've witnessed this myself. No man can profit."

Phineas took another step closer. She could feel his hot breath graze her sore skull. He said, "Let me guess. You've given up trying to kill yourself on the velocipede. So now you believe you're a crystal-ball gazer."

"Yes," Effy said quickly. "I ... I *can* see the future, and it's nothing but trouble."

"What are you getting at with your foolish gibberish?"

"The sapphire is cursed," shouted Effy. "It will bring you nothing but heartache like it did for Cuthbert. And look what happened to Madelene—now she's cursed."

Phineas hesitated. His bushy brows shot up. "Why are you telling *me* this?"

Effy refused to flinch under his smouldering glare. "I watched you spin three times before each circus act. You wear a rabbit's foot—all for good luck."

"Every ringmaster observes those rituals," Phineas said coolly. "Otherwise, the performers get skittish."

Effy looked at Phineas's puzzled face and it hit her. He was no more superstitious than she was. His little rituals had nothing to do with Rimaldi superstitions. She would not beat him at this game. Phineas was not afraid of any cursed sapphire.

Effy hung her head. "Isn't keeping my trust fund enough money for you?"

Then a peculiar thing happened. Phineas broke her gaze and staggered backwards.

"You think I'm stealing your trust fund?" Phineas sat on his bunk with a thud. "I sent for your trust fund so you could go back to school, the sooner the better, foolish child. You're certainly nothing but a sack of worries for me here."

Wasn't that what Effy had wanted all along? Why did her heart still feel as if it was tied to a bag of rocks? "But Balally ..."

"You think so low of me that I'd steal your trust fund, and then steal a sapphire from one of my own performers?" Phineas's shoulders slumped.

"How did you get the money for back wages and bonuses?" Effy was doing her best to keep up. If Phineas didn't steal the sapphire, then ... then ... She became so lost in this puzzle, Effy almost missed Phineas's next words.

"I've sold the circus," Phineas said. He slumped his head on the table.

The tall man poked his head inside the door. "Sorry to interrupt, but the cook wants to know ..."

Before the tall man could finish his sentence, Effy ducked between him and the ringmaster and ran for the elephant pen. She climbed inside the pen and flopped on a bale of hay. More fat drops of rain fell and mixed with the hot, fat tears rolling down her cheeks. Effy's throat closed as she swallowed.

Think, Effy, *think.* Use your reason and stick to the facts. She held her hand in front of her and started counting fingers.

First finger: Cuthbert lost the ring when he'd gone inside the tent for only a moment.

Second finger: Balally hadn't made a sound, which she always did, even if she was greeting a friend.

Third finger: Cuthbert didn't see anyone near the pen when he searched for the ring.

Effy waggled her pinky finger. She had thoroughly searched the carnival grounds and the grass field. The ring went somewhere. It didn't disappear.

She looked up at the tree branches and remembered how Balally loved reaching up and plucking leaves, one by one. For a second, the setting sun tried bursting through the cloud cover. A single ray shone through the branches.

Among the golden leaves, a blue stone flashed in its light.

CHAPTER TWENTY-SIX

THE RIDE OF THE VALKYRIE

The bicycle leaned against the canvas wall of the circus tent. The circus workers ignored Effy. They were busy driving extra stakes into the flapping big top before the wind tore up the carnival ground. Sawdust flew everywhere, and Effy's eyes itched and burned. She jumped on the wooden bike and pedalled as fast as she could.

That dratted bike—its wooden wheels wobbled and stuck as rain began pelting down, turning the ground into mud.

"Where are you going?" shouted Madam Vadoma.

"She's riding like a Valkyrie straight out of the sky," said Miss Dot.

Effy gripped the handles of the velocipede as its wooden wheels dug into wet grass and muck. As she steered onto the path, wet leaves tumbled from the trees and stuck to her face. Soon her stockings were soaked from splashing through puddles.

Effy found that as long as she kept pedalling, she could keep her bike balanced. Gaining any worthwhile speed was the tricky part. She lumbered along the rutted trail until it forked into two pathways. Effy kept pedalling until she pulled up at the railway station. A steam whistle blew in the distance, and Effy pushed the last ounce of her strength into those pedals.

In a hiss of steam and the squeal of metal against metal, the train pulled into the station. Charcoal smoke poured between the wheels and the train track.

Stop!" Effy rode up to the elephant wagon. "Don't load Balally onto the boxcar." She dropped the heavy bicycle and bent over, trying to catch her breath.

"It's no use," Cuthbert said wearily. He stood in the rain beside the wagon. His face was streaked with dust and tears. "I ... I've tried everything to talk them out of sending Balally away."

"But—" Effy wheezed.

"Sorry, nephew. But our beautiful Balally is lost to us now." Mr. Amal climbed down from the wagon, lifted his hand, and rested it on Cuthbert's shoulder.

Effy plucked the sapphire ring from her pocket. "I think our thief was Balally herself. She must have spotted the shiny trinket on the stool and picked it up with her trunk. Then she left it hanging on a branch above the pen."

The sapphire's light lit the uncle's face. He grinned. Effy handed Mr. Amal his ring. He immediately flashed it under the noses of the workmen. "Hold off, good gentlemen, and let me secure a kingly sum for this ring. I can reward you."

The townsman with the handlebar moustache hesitated in the middle of climbing back into the wagon. He eyed the ring. "It looks purty, but how do I know what it's worth?"

"I can tell you," said another man. He walked from the waiting area to the train platform. "There's a jeweller in town, and I was assisting him. He's been here settling an estate."

He pulled a jewellers loupe out of the pocket of his wrinkled jacket and placed it on his eye. He stared at the ring. His other eye widened. "This is a doozy, worth a fortune. Get yourself to the town's bank lickety-split. The jeweller's packing up and heading out on this train."

"Cuthbert, you need to do this." The uncle sat on a nearby bench. "I cannot," he wheezed, "catch my breath."

"Climb on the back of my bicycle," Effy told Cuthbert. "We'll ride to town."

Cuthbert shook his head. "I've seen you ride. I want to stay in one piece. Uncle, we need more time."

The old elephant handler looked up at the workers in the wagon. "There will be a tidy bonus for you, once I sell the ring. Just don't load my elephant on the train."

The other townsman jumped off the wagon and tipped his cap. "At your service, Mister."

"Not so fast," said the man with the handlebar moustache. "This elephant is supposed to go out on this train in fifty minutes. I've got the papers that say so." A sly look crossed his brow. "But if actual money greased my hand, I suppose I could take a bit of time loading her in the box car. But hurry."

Lightning lit the sky with blinding whiteness. Then thunder crashed, splitting Effy's ears. Balally thrashed against her chains, pulling one out, and she knocked one side of the wagon down in an angry stomp.

"We need to get my elephant under cover," said Mr. Amal.

"You don't have to tell me twice," said the man with the moustache.

"Effy, we'd better hurry." With his mouth set in a line of grim determination, Cuthbert climbed on the back of her bicycle.

Effy ignored the aches in every square inch of her body and started pedalling. Cuthbert only gasped once as they wobbled onto the path. Looking up, fat raindrops splattered against her face. A fork of lightning lit up the darkening sky, and thunder crashed. Effy's ears rang.

Effy pedalled toward the sinking sun that flushed like a splotch of blood in the cloud-covered sky. Her legs strained against the stiff block pedals. Her lungs stung as every breath burned its way down. Gradually, the dirt road widened, and the velocipede gained more speed, as the wheels spat up gravel and stones instead of muck.

Small cedar-shake houses dotted the street and then gave way to a few brick buildings ahead. People gathered at their white picket fences. She spotted Sofia, who waved to her as she rode by.

"That bicycle has plum set you free," Sofia hollered. Then she began running after them. Effy checked over her shoulder and let out a surprised squawk. She and Cuthbert had gathered their own parade along the way. In the distance, she saw a horse-drawn circus wagon closing in. Madame Vadoma, Miss Mabel, Mr. Jefferson, and, Effy's eyes widened, Phineas, were waving frantically.

Effy pedalled past the general store, past a church with a steeple, and past a barber shop with a wooden sign in the window, saying: TEETH PULLED; BULLET REMOVAL; WHISKY; AND A SHAVE FOR FIVE CENTS. When they reached the bank, Effy dropped the bicycle with a hard crash.

Trees surrounded the building, and their thrashing branches shook. Leaves scattered in the rising wind. The sun was barely a white wisp in the dark grey horizon. Effy and Cuthbert burst through the heavy oak doors of the bank.

A man at the counter in a bowler hat and checkered suit snapped shut his leather case.

Effy caught her breath. "Are you the jeweller who's leaving town?"

The man's cigar wobbled in his mouth. "I am." He scowled at Effy. "But I'm done here. I have a train to catch."

Cuthbert pulled the star sapphire out of his deep pocket and placed it on the marble counter. The jeweller's bushy grey eyebrows shot up.

"What have we got here," he said, as a puff of stinky cigar smoke blew in Effy's face.

CHAPTER TWENTY-SEVEN

SETTING THINGS RIGHT

Beneath the haze of cigar smoke, the star sapphire blinked under the new buzzing electric light. The star grew inside the blue gem, and when the sapphire blazed, Effy felt it was the most beautiful ring she'd ever laid eyes on. She also felt dizzy, and she lurched and grabbed a railing.

"This is a very valuable ring," Effy sputtered between coughs.

"It's a blue star sapphire," Cuthbert said. "It was found in Ceylon, and its star is perfectly formed. So it's very valuable."

"Like I said," Effy added.

"So you did." The jeweller looked impressed, with the sapphire, not with Effy in particular. He picked up the star sapphire and stared at it through the magnifying glass of his jewellers loupe.

"So, where did a little boy and girl get such a fancy ring?" He eyed them suspiciously.

Effy pulled her gaze away from the banker's clock on the wall—tick tock—time was running out. "Why do you want to know?" she asked in her best imitation of Aunt Ada's disapproving voice.

"Nuthin', never mind, snoopy questions are bad for business." The jeweller took the ring behind a glass door while Cuthbert and Effy waited … and waited. The manager and a curious bank clerk came out of their offices and stood by the counter. The clock kept ticking forward, and with every minute, Balally would be led toward the train—the poor elephant must be terrified. Also, each ticking minute they were trying to save Balally, Madelene and her family was sitting on hard benches in the courthouse, or worse, staring out at the world from behind bars.

Effy hoped the Yolandas could hang on a while longer. "Save Balally," Madelene had told her. That's what Effy would do first—she swayed and grabbed the edge of the counter. If only the room would stop spinning.

Finally, the jeweller came back.

"Some star sapphires *are* cursed," he said flatly. He put the star sapphire on the marble counter and shoved it toward Effy and Cuthbert.

"Nonsense," said Effy.

"I told you," Cuthbert whispered in Effy's ear.

"Just because somebody believes it, doesn't make it so," Effy shot back.

"Not that *I'm* superstitious," said the jeweller in the bowler hat, "but a cursed ring doesn't bring as good a return on my investment." He shook his head, but his eyes held a greedy gleam, and he kept a steady gaze on Cuthbert's ring.

The jeweller let out a puff of stinky cigar smoke, and the cigar wobbled between his lips as he said, "I'll pay you fifty dollars. That's my best offer under the likely cursed circumstances."

Effy knew he was just trying to drive a hard bargain.

"That's not the gem's worth," said Cuthbert. He turned to Effy. "We can't pay our passage *and* buy our elephant back from the circus.

A customer reached from behind and rang the service bell. Effy refused to take her eyes off the slippery jeweller when the customer hit the bell again, harder. The jeweller looked up and paled. The cigar slipped from his mouth and fell on the marble floor.

"Perhaps I can make you a better offer." This time the jeweller sounded as if his words had been dipped in honey.

Effy turned around. Phineas stood right behind her, his ringmaster's whip belted against his thigh. Mr. Jefferson stood behind him. Miss Mabel and Madam Vadoma and Miss Dot had gathered at the open door. Beyond the door, Effy spotted Sophia and Mrs. Winterbottom, and perhaps half the town.

As soon as the jeweller handed Cuthbert an envelope of cash, the train whistle blew. Cuthbert raced for the door. "We have to hurry."

Effy's trusty legs, which had pedalled her bicycle past the railway station and to the bank, gave up on her. She crumbled slowly toward the ground.

Phineas scooped her up, but Effy squirmed out of his arms. "We have to save Balally now. The train will be pulling out of the station any minute."

"Everyone, get in the wagon," bellowed Phineas.

Had Phineas just agreed with her, or was Effy twisting the words in her aching head? Certainly, everything else was circling around as if she was on a carousel. Effy was happy not to have to climb back on the bicycle. Her wobbly knees barely held true.

She swayed again. Madame Vadoma put a steadying arm on Effy as she climbed into the wagon. Effy brushed it away.

"You're right, Mabel," said Madame Vadoma, "this one's orneriness has put a rod up her backbone. She's as determined as they come, her father through and through."

"No," said Miss Dot. "Effy is stubborn, but she hasn't locked her heart away in a cash box."

Phineas harrumphed, but Miss Dot glared back at him. Then she and Cuthbert, Madame Vadoma, Mr. Jefferson, and Miss Mabel all piled in the wagon behind Effy. Phineas shook the reins and the wagon lurched forward. Effy leaned into the ample shoulder of Miss Mabel, who patted her arm, saying, "There, there, dearie. You look completely spent."

As if Effy was the one in need of any comfort. All she could see behind her closed eyes was Balally flailing her trunk and trumpeting for help. The train whistle shrieked. As they pulled up to the train platform, Effy's heart leaped into her throat. The townsmen were loading Balally into a boxcar. Balally thrashed against her chains, her eyes rolled back.

"No!" Effy's heart banged in her chest, and she suddenly found a new spurt of energy. She and Cuthbert jumped out of the wagon and hit the ground before the wagon wheels had even stopped spinning. They raced toward the men.

"We have the money to ship Balally back to Ceylon." Effy waved her arms. Cuthbert pulled a handful of dollar bills out of the envelope and waved them, which caught the moustache man's attention.

"Hold off, now!" he shouted to the other men.

The train conductor looked at his pocket watch and blew his whistle several times. "All aboard or be left in the dust." When nobody moved, he glared at them.

Phineas stepped up. "There have been terrible train accidents when an elephant is spooked. You might want to delay for a few minutes."

Effy recognized the pesky conductor. He was all about the rules. She pointed to Phineas and said, "You'd best listen to my father."

The conductor's eyes darted from Phineas to Effy and back again. "He really does carry a whip," said the conductor, in a shaky voice.

He scurried off to notify the engineer.

"We sold the sapphire, Uncle. We can save Balally and break the curse." Cuthbert handed the money envelope over to his uncle.

"There was no curse," Effy said under her breath and to no one in particular.

"You did say something about a bonus if we forget

about these papers?" the townsman in the hat asked.

The man with the handlebar moustache elbowed him in the ear. "Er, not that we can be bribed." He gulped.

Effy turned around. Phineas stood behind her, his arms crossed.

"You don't have to worry, the ringmaster is here to save Balally," said Effy. "He'll take care of this."

Phineas widened his eyes. "Well, I suppose I will. Load the elephant onto the wagon and take her back to the circus, until I sign over her papers." He turned to Cuthbert's uncle. "I'm sure Mr. Amal and I can agree on a price."

"No." Effy stepped between the handler and Phineas. "They shouldn't have to pay a penny to get their elephant back."

Phineas stared at her for several heartbeats. He sighed. "I suppose not paying the elephant's keep any longer will be compensation enough. That beast ate its weight in hay every livelong day."

Mr. Amal hugged the ringmaster. Phineas almost dropped to the ground in surprise. He quickly pulled out of the embrace, but Effy saw his lips twitch in an upward motion.

"The curse truly is broken," Cuthbert's uncle told Effy, "whether or not you believe in curses."

Something had changed, this was true. Effy decided it was what Aunt Ada always called a rare moment of people coming together.

Cuthbert rushed to calm Balally as they backed her away from the boxcar.

"We must get her well away and fast," said the old handler. "A train in motion is a terrifying thing for an elephant to behold."

Because it's like a great giant beast, thought Effy. *That belches steam and roars.*

They quickly loaded Balally onto the wagon. Cuthbert patted his friend's trunk and told her, "Just a little longer, girl, and soon you will never be in chains again. You will roam where your heart desires. You will be free."

Free. Madelene! Effy smacked her forehead. "Ouch. We have to get back to the jail and fetch the Great Yolandas."

Once more, Effy insisted on accompanying Phineas as he and the other performers bombarded the constable's office and demanded the release of their fellow performers. As Effy waited on the hard bench in the constabulary, Miss Mabel put a cool hand on her brow.

"This girl's running a fever," she told Phineas. He frowned.

When Madelene and her brother and their mother strode in, Effy noted the jaunty thrust of Madelene's jaw, and how she squared her shoulders and marched triumphantly. "Did you save Balally?" she asked.

Effy managed to nod, even though nothing else on her body seemed to be cooperating any longer.

"Told you we didn't steal anything," Madelene snapped back at the constable, once she was safely out the door.

Effy let Phineas help her into the wagon. The others all crammed together, so he could lay her down on something soft. Miss Mabel tucked a blanket under her chin.

Madelene looked at Effy and shrugged. "Course you get all the attention, ringmaster's daughter, even though I've been locked behind bars." But she grabbed Effy's hand and held on tightly.

"What about the circus? What will you do now?" Effy could only croak. All her hollering had left her throat raw.

"You let me worry on that, daughter," Phineas said into her ear. "You've already done more than anyone could."

Through the layers of fog that gathered in Effy's brain, she realized Phineas had called her *daughter*.

CHAPTER TWENTY-EIGHT
ONE TRUE PURPOSE?

Effy finished packing her embroidered bag. She left behind her performance costume, which, after all her cutting and sewing, would likely be used for rags. The gold sash: *Equality for All* was the last item to go inside. She fastened the bag's clasp. Straightening her practical brown frock, she stuffed her long braid under her straw boater's hat. When Effy opened her caravan's door, she plopped her bag on the top step and looked around.

The big top was collapsing as circus workers removed the tent poles. The wagon carts had been closed and locked. Willy, who still hadn't overcome his fear of heights, was raking the sawdust into piles. All the banners and gaslights and colourful flags had been removed. Effy marvelled at how quickly the circus grounds had turned back into a farmer's field.

Leaving her bag on the step, Effy made her way to the cook's tent, which hadn't been taken down yet. Miss

Mabel and Madam Vadoma sat on a bench and were enjoying cups of coffee. Both coffee and spare time had been rare as oranges in the circus. Madam Vadoma clapped her hands.

"Here she is, up and around, looking healthy as a lamb in spring." Madam Vadoma smiled. "Just as I predicted."

Effy surprised herself when she hugged Madam Vadoma. By the look of her face, Madam Vadoma was also surprised. But she hugged Effy back—fiercely.

"I'm ... going to miss everyone so." To Effy's annoyance, a tear trickled down her cheek. She brushed it away.

"And us you. Without you, how will we manage to keep Phineas distracted and out of our hair?" Madam Vadoma laughed, but when she noticed Effy's watery eyes, she patted her arm. "There now. We'll be seeing you regularly. Most of us are just going to be in the next town with Phineas."

Effy sniffed. "I know." Phineas would be setting up a variety theatre. Madam Vadoma would be the mesmerist and busy herself with reading people's minds and palms; Jacque would become the funambulist, walking tightropes across the stage; and Yolanda would still swing from a trapeze. Miss Dot, on the other hand, wished to try her hand at singing.

"Come here," said Miss Mabel, setting her tin cup on the wood table. Effy stepped into Miss Mabel's arms. "You know we'll be returning this spring with Mr. Jefferson's carnival of amusement rides," said Miss Mabel. Her face softened. "Who wouldn't want a wedding in a town named Bridal Falls."

Mr. Jefferson wasn't interested in theatre. He liked machines, and had become fascinated with a new ride called the gravity twisty-track. He was working on the startup of a newfangled roller coaster company.

Effy pulled away from Miss Mabel's comforting arms and forced a smile. "I'll not forget the wedding." She turned to Madame Vadoma. "And, of course, I'll come see the new show when it's up and running."

As she bid her goodbyes to the rest of the performers, she learned that when Phineas had finally paid up, he'd gained new respect by paying both the men and women equally.

It heartened Effy greatly that the women acrobats were taking up their cause of equality with their new circus, *Barnum & Bailey*. They'd be joining the other circus suffragists and would fight for equal pay there. Aunt Ada would never have seen that coming, but Effy's heart swelled with hope and pride for them.

Effy's joy dipped as she braced herself. This would be her hardest goodbye. She stopped at the elephant pen where Balally chirped a friendly greeting.

Balally reached out with her trunk. First Effy patted it, and then she reached in her pocket and handed Balally a crisp autumn apple. It was gone in a crunch.

"Effy, I haven't told you yet." Cuthbert hurried toward her.

"I'm guessing this is good news." Effy smiled back. "Or are you just happy because I haven't brought my bicycle."

Cuthbert laughed. "There was enough money left after we booked our passage, so I can go to engineering school."

He frowned and patted Balally's trunk. "Of course, I won't leave Ceylon until Uncle and Balally are settled in the elephant sanctuary, and Balally is happy with all her new elephant friends."

Effy hugged Cuthbert goodbye. "I will miss you both more than I can ever say." She kept swallowing but it was no good. Her throat felt too thick.

"But that's not all the good news," Cuthbert said brightly. "Mr. Jefferson has offered me a job in his new company when I become an engineer."

"That's wonderful, Cuthbert!" Effy said.

She hoped she could spend more time with her

friends, but it wasn't long before Mr. Jefferson called her over. It was time to leave. After patting Balally one more time, she swore the elephant waved goodbye.

Madelene was waiting for Effy at the caravan. "Too bad we're leaving," she said. Madelene looked genuinely sad. "For an uppity girl and a guttersnipe girl, we were starting to fit in here."

No praise could have been higher. Effy hoisted her bag off the step and, lacing her arm in Madelene's, they strode to the entrance of the circus. Phineas stood with the small group of people Effy had come to think of as her family. A horse-drawn carriage approached from a distance.

Phineas took out a pocket watch and glanced at the time. "They are prompt," he said approvingly. Then he turned to Effy. "I am glad to see you're finally looking fit as a fiddle."

"Thank you, sir," Effy said politely.

Madame Vadoma leaned over and whispered into Effy's ear. "Aren't you going to hug your father goodbye?"

Effy stared straight ahead. Besides helping Balally and Cuthbert, Phineas had helped everyone find work after he sold the Great Rimaldi Circus. He'd proven he was not a scoundrel or a flimflammer. Those were good things, wonderful things, but standing before him, it was as if Effy's arms were glued to her sides. Not that it mattered—Phineas's own arms were behind his back.

"Until spring," said Mr. Jefferson. He stepped closer and surprised Effy with a peck on the cheek. Effy had no trouble hugging him.

"For the wedding," Miss Mabel said again, stroking her shiny beard.

"I trust you'll be writing me letters from your new school," said Phineas.

Effy nodded. "Mrs. Winterbottom insists that we write weekly."

Sofia's mother, Mrs. Winterbottom, had been the woman in town selling off her estate. She was starting a new school. "Coeducational," Sofia had told Effy with bubbling delight.

"Because colleges will find it harder to turn down girls when they accept boys' applications from the same school," Mrs. Winterbottom had explained to Phineas. The girls could be boarding students, and she'd readily offered Effy a space. Mrs. Winterbottom had told Phineas she'd be proud to have such a modern-thinking girl as Effy attend her school.

As the carriage pulled to a stop, Madelene took her own bag from her mother and stood beside Effy. "My mother told me to thank you both again for the scholarship," she said to Effy and Phineas.

Effy had asked Phineas if her trust fund would also allow a scholarship in Aunt Ada's name. Phineas had waggled his eyebrows and said there'd been enough money that she could sponsor a new girl every year, if that's what she wanted. Effy was sure it was exactly what her aunt would have wished.

The carriage door opened, and Sofia tumbled out first, her blond ringlets bouncing, and her pink ribbons flying. "I knew we would be friends forever when I found that hairpin on the train," she told Effy.

Sofia scooped Madelene's bag from her, and a sly smile crossed her face. "Just so you know," Sofia's eyes flashed wickedly, "the first boys will begin school tomorrow morning. Who would have thought there would be so much to look forward to with school?"

Madelene rolled her eyes but only for Effy to see.

Mrs. Winterbottom poked her head out of the carriage. "Sofia," she said, with some exasperation, "not another word about boys or *you* will attend that girls finishing school."

Sofia's eyes widened in alarm. "Not another word, Mama, I promise." As she climbed back inside the carriage with Madelene, she said, "In that school, it's only girls and everyone dresses like nuns."

"Sofia," Mrs. Winterbottom scolded.

"Goodbye, daughter," said Phineas. He handed Effy a bouquet of flowers that he'd been holding behind his back.

White poppies: S*orrow. I'm sorry. I'll never forget you.*

Yellow roses: *I'm asking for forgiveness.*

Effy dropped her bag and ran into her father's arms. "I will miss you, Poppa."

"That's unlikely," her poppa said gruffly. "But I'll hold you to that. I expect a visit every school holiday, once I set up our acts in that new theatre."

Effy promised. Surprised to be blinking back tears, she stepped into the carriage, turned, and waved, vowing to carry forward Aunt Ada's one true purpose. She would help blaze a path for more girls to go to college. In order to do that, she'd need to be heard, and she'd need to be loud.

And then, surely, there would be other paths to blaze—Effy would need to be loud for everyone.

Hoping Aunt Ada wouldn't have been too disappointed, Effy realized she was never going to be a girl with one true purpose after all.

She was going to be a girl with many purposes.

AUTHOR'S NOTE

There was a time in Canada when only men—not women—were allowed to vote in political elections. The right to vote—and other things related to equality for women—took time and effort to achieve.

Women organized and lobbied under activists including Emily Stowe. They also joined global organizations such as the Woman's Christian Temperance Union. During the First World War, some women were allowed to vote. This opened the door. Canada granted women the right to vote in 1918, but their fight wasn't over. It would take years to achieve universal suffrage where all women received voting rights.

Many of the people Effy mentions in this novel are real, historical figures. Emily Roebling, Emily Stowe and her daughter, and Clara Brett Martin, were all women of the time.

At the turn of the 20th century, circuses became

strongholds for the suffragist movement, demonstrating equality for women. Female performers drove home the message that women weren't frail, and could match and even outmatch the male performers with feats of derring-do. Circus workers were one of the earliest groups to demand equal pay for equal work.

In an earlier era, small travelling circuses regularly crossed North America to entertain family audiences. Eventually, small travelling circuses—such as the fictional one owned by Effy's father—were under pressure to compete with larger "three ring" circuses that could present hundreds of animals and trainloads of top circus acts. The history of elephants and the early circus is heartbreaking.

With the support of the animal rights activists, many countries and cities have banned wild animal acts, including many Canadian cities. Cirque du Soleil, a Canadian entertainment company, led the way for dazzling circus entertainment that is animal free. Ringling Bros. and Barnum & Bailey are returning with human acts only. Many of Ringling's former elephants were moved to a 135-acre sanctuary: whiteoakwildlife.org in Florida, where the elephants wander the woods and bathe in deep ponds. Balally would have loved it there.

Women in earlier times were not encouraged to be independent. Riding velocipedes, later called bicycles, was thought of as an activity only for men. The medical world had proclaimed women as too frail, and, in addition, women's clothing was too restrictive for riding. Suffragists at the time, however, decided a bicycle was a way to set women free. For the first time, women began wearing pants in public, as skirts and petticoats would catch on pedals and gears. Women in trousers raised a lot of eyebrows, but they kept on pedalling and organizing toward equality.

ACKNOWLEDGMENTS

Thank you to my editor, Beverley Brenna, who has been a wonderful collaborator. Also, thanks to Penny Hozy for her added insight, and to everyone at Red Deer Press for the hard work and magic it took to turn my manuscript into a book. Much appreciation to my trusted early readers, Janine Cross and Ari Goelman, and thank you to Gina McMurchy-Barber, Patricia Morrison, and Mary Reid for the polish. As always, much love and appreciation to John, Alec, and Joey.

PHOTO: JOHN DEMEULEMEESTER

For more information, please see www.lindademeulemeester.com
or www.grimhill.com

LINDA DEMEULEMEESTER

This is your first historical fiction title, although you have other books that engage adventure. What inspired you to set this story in another time period?

I loved historical adventures as a younger reader, and I still do. The stories I named in the book—such as *Swiss Family Robinson, Black Beauty,* and "The Rime of the Ancient Mariner"—were all stories I discovered at ten or eleven years old. I went on to read books about ancient Egypt, Roman times, Medieval times—their backdrops as strange and fascinating as stories with fantastical settings.

For *Ephemia Rimaldi,* specifically, I had started a story about a curse and about a girl travelling back in time. The story didn't work. But one section set in a circus at the turn of the century wouldn't leave my imagination. It became the setting of this new book.

How did you complete the research necessary for this story—by reading and taking jot notes ahead of time, or by looking into particular subjects as you went along?

I research as I go along. Let's put it this way: when I had a job as a library clerk, I wasn't very efficient. I couldn't put one book back in the stacks without pulling out two others and flipping through them. The same is with research—I'd keep going and not get any writing done.

Once I knew my character, an unconventional girl for her time, I began looking into early circuses. I read a lot of magazine articles—*Life and Times Magazine* had published issues on circuses around this time, and I snapped them up. They were wonderful because they had firsthand accounts from interviews with circus performers—what social studies teachers call "primary sources." There are plenty of websites about circus specifics on the Internet, which I dived into—these are called "secondary sources."

That's when I stumbled on the fact that the circus performers were one of the earliest groups to organize for equal pay. Not only did that give me the idea for beginning my story with a suffragist march, but it led me to read about many brave women in those earlier times.

Great historical fiction achieves two things simultaneously. It conveys a historical time and place, while making its characters engaging for today's readers. What were you consciously doing to make sure audiences found Effy entirely appealing and relatable?

I wrote for my eleven- and twelve-year-old self, so the kernels of this story are wrapped in adventure and spiced with a hint of the unknown—is there a curse or not? Is superstition mystical or coincidental? I particularly loved stories that had to convince me ... or even better, left it for me to decide myself.

Some writers start with a plot and create characters from there, while other writers begin with a character. How did this story unfold for you?

Ephemia Rimaldi: Circus Performer Extraordinaire began with a character that hovered in my imagination and refused to leave: a girl who thoroughly vexed her father, the ringmaster of a circus. Who was this girl? Why was she so obstinate? What shaped her to defy the attitudes of her time? I had to write about her.

In conjuring Ephemia, I wanted her inspired by strong women. Her great-aunt was fashioned after stoic and independent literary characters such as Marilla from *Anne of Green Gables*, and by real women of that time. Great-aunt Ada was also influenced by my own grandmother who, born on a farm on the prairies, had become an accountant and the western manager of a large company by the end of the Second World War—an accomplishment that defied a lot of norms.

I have always been intrigued by how travelling circuses from that era could show two sides: one of cruelty and one of tolerance. Ephemia has a growing awareness of the strange world she's entered. She begins to question other lines that are drawn in her society. Animals, she discovers, are beautiful and complex. Circus people that others look down upon are no different from herself, except in opportunity. She discovers common ground with the rich girl she's met on the train, and the aerialist from a traveller's family, as well as the elephant handler who has come from so far away.

Is this story completely fiction, or are there any true stories from your family woven into its fabric?
A kernel for the circus story derives from a tale my grandmother told me. When I was a girl, my brother and

I loved all her stories about the olden days. This one was about her attending the first Pacific National Exhibition parade in 1910. She was nine years old, and when an elephant turned the corner and came toward her, my grandmother fainted. Nothing in the early 20th century, certainly not pictures, had prepared her for the enormity of that majestic creature. This inspired me for the early scenes with Ephemia, when she arrives at the circus and first encounters the elephant, Balally. She comes to appreciate what an amazing creature the elephant is. This is why she's swiftly on board for trying to save her.

Did you enjoy writing when you were a child? What advice do you have for young aspiring writers who might be reading this book?

My mother surprised me a few years ago by showing me the first books I wrote when I was six or seven. I couldn't believe she'd kept them. One was a story about a cat and its instincts. The other story, carefully folded and stapled, was an illustrated tale about a princess who ate a lot of blackberries—in the story, she kept popping them into her mouth.

As for advice to young writers, it is the same advice I'm sure they've already heard because it's so true. Read,

read a lot, read everything. I'd also say do interesting things—go kayaking, ride a horse, build a fort or a go-cart—get involved in anything creative and fun. You never know when that experience will come in handy with one of your stories.